"My Son Is Go[...]
My Roof. You Can Either Help
Or Get Out Of The Way."

"How am I supposed to make all these arrangements? Get everything packed?"

"Don't worry about packing. I can pay for everything you and Joel could need or want."

Nicole shook her head. "You just don't understand. Security doesn't always come from money and things. It comes from people and familiarity."

"I'll be that person for Joel. My home will become that place for him, too." He paused three heartbeats. "Are you coming or not?"

"You've given me no choice."

"You're valuable to my son. I'll make sure you're well rewarded financially."

"I don't want your money," she told him.

Rafe shrugged. "My private jet will take us to Miami. Be ready."

Despite her huge doubts about Rafe's ability to be a

Dear Reader,

I love a self-made man. All that strength, determination and confidence make this girl weak in the knees!

I'm thrilled to present three irresistible self-made men in my new series, THE MEDICI MEN. During a trip to Italy I was inspired by the tales of the famous Medici family. In my trilogy, the Medici brothers were torn apart as children, and finding their way back to believing in love takes the help of some strong women. In *From Playboy to Papa!* we meet sexy, wealthy Rafe Medici. When he learns he has a young son, he's determined to make up for lost time. Nicole Livingstone may be giving Rafe daddy lessons, but Rafe and Nicole quickly start giving each other lessons in love. Both Rafe and Nicole have secrets in their pasts that could destroy their chance for a happy family, so their love will need to be stronger than their secrets. I hope you enjoy the exciting ride of this heart-tugging love story.

I love to hear from readers and would love to hear your thoughts about Rafe. Please write me at leannebbb@aol.com and visit my Web site, www.leannebanks.com.

All the best,

Leanne Banks

LEANNE BANKS

FROM PLAYBOY TO PAPA!

Published by Silhouette Books

America's Publisher of Contemporary Romance

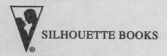

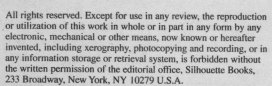

SILHOUETTE BOOKS

ISBN-13: 978-0-373-73000-1

FROM PLAYBOY TO PAPA!

Recycling programs
for this product may
not exist in your area.

Visit Silhouette Books at www.eHarlequin.com

Printed in U.S.A.

Books by Leanne Banks

Silhouette Desire

Royal Dad #1400
Tall, Dark & Royal #1412
His Majesty, M.D. #1435
The Playboy & Plain Jane #1483
Princess in His Bed #1515
Between Duty and Desire #1599
Shocking the Senator #1621
Billionaire's Proposition #1699
†*Bedded by the Billionaire* #1863
†*Billionaire's Marriage Bargain* #1886
Blackmailed Into a Fake Engagement #1916
†*Billionaire Extraordinaire* #1939
**From Playboy to Papa!* #1987

*The Royal Dumonts
†The Billionaires Club
**The Medici Men

LEANNE BANKS

is a *New York Times* and *USA TODAY* bestselling author who is surprised every time she realizes how many books she has written. Leanne loves chocolate, the beach and new adventures. To name a few, Leanne has ridden on an elephant, stood on an ostrich egg (no, it didn't break), gone parasailing and indoor skydiving. Leanne loves writing romance because she believes in the power and magic of love. She lives in Virginia with her family and her four-and-a-half-pound Pomeranian named Bijou. Visit her Web site at www.leannebanks.com.

This book is dedicated to my Italian trip cohorts in adventure and calamity, Tony, Ann and Ray, Terri and David. Catching a train was never so traumatic. Thank God for laughter, good friends, wine and chocolate gelato....

Prologue

It was 1 a.m. and the Medici brothers were ringing in the New Year with a bottle of Scotch and a game of pool. For once, Rafe was finally winning against his older brother Damien. His younger brother Michael, however was nipping at his heels.

"Let's wrap this up," Damien said, taking a shot and missing in his haste.

"Anxious to get back to your bride?" Rafe asked, goading him.

"She should be out of the shower by now," Damien said, a rare smile playing on his lips. "I plan to start the New Year off right."

"I never thought you'd let a woman come between you and beating me at pool," Rafe said, sinking a ball into the corner pocket.

"You're just jealous because you don't have a woman like Emma waiting for you," Damien retorted.

Rafe couldn't prevent a stab of regret. Ever since his disastrous romance with Tabitha Livingstone, he hadn't let a woman get under his skin. Rafe scratched his next shot and muttered under his breath.

"He's right about that," Michael said and shot his ball into the hole. "Yes," he said in triumph. He lined up his next shot and missed.

Damien glanced at his watch then looked at each of his brothers. He set down his cue and lifted his glass. "To both of you, may you find a woman half as fine as Emma this year." He took a sip and walked out of the room.

"Then I'll take the match." Rafe took the next shot and the next. Two more and he took the game.

"You won," Michael said.

"Yes, I did," Rafe said, but the taste of triumph wasn't nearly as sweet as he'd thought it would be.

"What do you want to do now?" Michael asked, looking as if he too felt at loose ends.

"Blackjack," Rafe said. "We may not be lucky in love, but I bet we can clean up in cash."

One

The photo in the newspaper sitting on the edge of the table distracted Rafe. The woman looked familiar. Pulling the newspaper closer, he took a second look and immediately identified the woman in the background of the photo. *Tabitha*.

His gut twisted as a half dozen emotions ambushed him. He knew that silky blond hair even though it was darker now, those sexy blue eyes, that body designed to make a man insane. And, boy, had she known how to use it. She'd wrapped him around her little finger then nearly squeezed the life out of him.

"So, this deal must be pretty big to drag you away from South Beach," his brother Michael said, tugging his attention back to the here and now.

"I don't mind traveling for the right customer. This client purchased two premium yachts and has some friends who want to lease." Rafe also didn't mind taking business away from Livingstone Yachts. In fact, he enjoyed every minute of torturing Tabitha's father, but he would keep that to himself. "What about you? Business looks good," Rafe said, glancing around the bar that his brother had turned into Atlanta's newest hotspot. He shook his head. "Michael's magic touch again."

Michael gave a rough chuckle. "You know better than that. It's me working my butt off."

"The way of the Medicis," Rafe said and thought of their oldest brother, Damien. "Damien would agree, but only to a certain extent since he's happily married now." His gaze was drawn again to the copy of The Atlanta-Constitution. He couldn't believe he'd foolishly considered a future with Tabitha.

"Hey, you're not listening to a word I'm saying," Michael said. "What are you looking at?"

Rafe narrowed his eyes, spotting the small boy standing beside Tabitha. Couldn't be more than four or five years old he thought. The lying woman had been seeing someone else at the same time she'd been burning up his bed, he thought in disgust. He'd caught her trying to seduce one of his clients.

"Do you know the guy in the wheelchair?" Michael asked.

"What—" Rafe paused and perused the article featuring a Marine veteran making a new life despite extensive disabilities. What the hell was Tabitha doing with him? She was a spoiled rich girl.

He frowned and studied the photo again. The little boy had brown, curly hair and stood shyly beside her leg. Rafe did the math and cold realization rushed through him. The boy looked like a Medici. Despite the fact that she was a cheater, he could be his son.

"Rafe, you're acting weird as hell," his brother said, his voice tinged with alarm.

"Yeah, well—" He shook his head and pointed to the article. "You know where this place is?"

Michael lifted his brow. "Yeah, not the nicest neighborhood in town. You probably don't want to spend a lot of time there after dark."

Rafe glanced at his watch. Eleven o'clock. Damn. He clenched his fist. He would find out if he had a son or not.

"What's going on?" Michael asked.

"I'm not sure, but I'm damn well going to find out first thing in the morning."

Nicole Livingstone pulled her coat around her body more tightly to ward off the January weather. Even though Atlanta was in the South, winter temperatures could dip into the thirties. She headed for her car, noticing a tall, handsome man walking along the same sidewalk toward her.

If she'd been the type to flirt, now would be the time. The man's broad shoulders were encased in a black leather jacket and he walked with a powerful and purposeful gait. His dark hair was tousled by the wind. Strong eyebrows framed his dark eyes. His cheeks held a tinge of color from the chill. The only downside was that his full mouth was set in a straight hard line, as if he were displeased and going to do something about it.

She averted her gaze.

"Tabitha," the man said, stopping in front of her. "Tabitha Livingstone."

Nicole whipped her gaze up to meet his, stunned that he would know her sister's name. "I'm not—"

"Don't try to fool me," he said. "You and I knew each other very well."

Nicole took a short breath, caught between disappointment and trepidation. Being mistaken for her twin had happened to her too many times to count, but not since her sister had died. The problem was that Nicole was never sure exactly how Tabitha had treated the person confronting her. Since her sister had died a few years ago, hearing the mistake came as a shock.

"My name is Nicole Livingstone. I'm Tabitha's twin."

She watched the man digest the news. Disbelief, then confusion crossed his face. "She never told me about a twin."

Nicole's uneasy laugh stuck in her throat. "She liked to keep it a surprise, so if she ever needed to refer to her evil twin…"

"Hmm," he said, his brow furrowing. He rubbed his chin. "Where is she?"

Nicole bit her lip. A stab of pain took her by surprise. Just when she thought she'd adjusted to the loss of her sister, she found out she hadn't. "She died three years ago."

His eyes widened in shock. "I didn't know."

She nodded. "She got a terrible infection and the doctors couldn't help her. People thought she was so headstrong that she could survive anything. It was a huge shock to us."

"I'm very sorry for your loss," he said, but she saw a hardness in his eyes. He extended his hand to her.

She took it and was immediately struck by his warmth and strength. His hand felt good around hers. "Thank you. And you are?"

"Rafe," he said. "Rafe Medici."

The world seemed to tilt sideways. Her heart hammered

in her chest as if someone had set off a fire alarm inside her. It took a moment for her to remove her hand from his.

She needed to get away from him. As fast as she possibly could. She took a deep breath and stepped backward. "Thank you again. Good-bye."

She started to walk around him, but he brushed her arm with his hand. Biting the inside of her lip, she paused and looked at the space between his eyes instead of meeting his gaze.

"In the newspaper, I saw a photograph of you with a child. Was he Tabitha's?"

"He's mine," she said, feeling her blood rush to her head. "Joel is mine."

"Did Tabitha have a child before she died?"

"Joel is mine. I need to go," she said and walked down the sidewalk to her Camry Hybrid parked in the lot. Her heart pounding a mile a minute, she unlocked the door and slid inside. She started to close the door, but Rafe Medici appeared beside her and caught it.

"Mr. Medici," she said, terror whipping through her.

"My father died when I was very young. It was a terrible loss. I would not want that for a son of mine."

The humanity in the man's expression caught her off guard. Her sister had described him as possessing a monster ego. Nicole shot a look at the large hand that prevented her departure. "Please step away from my vehicle. I need to leave," she managed in a voice she'd developed to freeze out arguments with uncooperative healthcare agencies.

She felt his assessing gaze as he slowly moved his hand. Not easily intimidated. Why should she be surprised? He stood over a half foot taller than her and with those wide shoulders and well-developed muscles she'd glimpsed as his jacket swung open, he could probably bench press three of her.

"Later," he said.

Nicole pulled her door shut and peeled out of the parking lot. *Later.* She certainly hoped not.

Now that Joel was ready to turn four, she'd thought they were in the clear. After all, there'd been no sign of Rafe Medici at her sister's funeral. No flowers. Nothing. Droplets of cold sweat forming on her skin, she exited on to the interstate, her mind whirling.

Nicole maintained a low profile. It had been easy for her. Tabitha had been the flashy one, and that had been fine with Nicole. Now, after all this time, she'd taken Joel to meet one of her patient clients to see his dinosaur model collection. A reporter writing stories about disabled veterans had surprised them and captured the three of them in a photograph, which had been published in the newspaper. Of all the dumb luck.

Clenching her fingers over the steering wheel, she wondered if she should take Joel and leave immediately. He was a shy little guy, though, and seemed to be flourishing in his pre-school class.

She remembered the look of determination on Rafe's face and shuddered. She considered her options. Her mother lived on the other side of the world—France, in fact. Nicole and Joel could disappear there, at least for a while. Her mother, however, led an active social life and having a preschooler around would cramp her style.

Tabitha would have turned to their father and performed a butter-him-up act worthy of an Oscar in order to get money from him. Nicole limited her involvement with her father as much as possible. After what he had done…

She took a deep breath to calm herself. She'd always been told she was the practical twin. Something would come to her. No matter what, she would protect Joel at all costs.

She was lying, Rafe thought as he watched her tear out of the parking lot. He felt a tingling sensation in his left hand that had served as a warning throughout his life. The woman would be trouble. Perhaps more trouble than Tabitha had been. If that were possible.

Tabitha had acted as if she'd enjoyed living with him, but soon enough he'd learned that all she wanted from him was his money. To this day, he didn't understand her greed. After all, her father was very wealthy. He remembered the way she'd begged him to let her sell a few of his yachts. He'd indulged her, secretly enjoying the fact that he was one-upping the mighty Conrad Livingstone via the man's daughter. The joke had backfired, though. She'd lied to him in order to pad her commission then tried to seduce one of his customers, a Spanish prince. Unsuccessfully.

Narrowing his eyes as the wind whipped around him, he walked toward his rental car. It shouldn't be difficult to find out the truth about Tabitha, Nicole and Joel.

Sliding into the car, he started the engine then dialed his brother.

"Hey, Rafe. What's up?" his brother Michael asked.

"I need the name of a good P.I. who is thorough, fast and discreet," he said.

"Okay. This wouldn't have anything to do with your bad mood last night, would it?"

"Maybe," Rafe said.

"Does this mean you'll be staying an extra night at my place?"

"Yeah, unless it's a problem," Rafe said.

"No, but I'll be gone most of the time. I just found a new business that I can buy cheap. You want to tell me what all this is about?" Michael asked.

"After I find out. Text me the phone number," Rafe said grimly. He wanted answers and he would get them.

After he received an initial report from his P.I., Rafe met with an attorney. "How much can Nicole Livingstone fight me for custody?"

The attorney shook his head. "She can fight, but unless she can prove you're an unfit parent, then she won't win. All you need is a paternity test that proves you're the boy's father. It's easy enough to get a court order for that."

Rafe thought about the years he'd been cheated from knowing his son, all because of the Livingstones. Bitterness surged through him. "These people have deceived me in the worst way. I want to take Joel away as soon as possible."

The attorney lifted his hand. "Not so fast."

"Why not?" Rafe demanded. "You just told me I can get custody without a problem."

"True," the man said. "But you have to remember the well-being of your son. Do you really want to rip him away from the one person he's known since birth? From all appearances, Nicole Livingstone has taken excellent care of Joel. Would you agree?"

"Yes," he said grudgingly.

"Legally, you may have the right to take him away so that he never sees Nicole again, but you need to consider what's best for Joel. How is he going to feel about being taken away from the woman he knows as his mother?"

Rafe felt a gut-wrenching twist at the thought. He had been

through a very similar experience—losing his parents and his family when he was a child, although not so young. The traumatic event had left him feeling lost for years. Despite his grudge against the Livingstones, he had to concede that Nicole Livingstone had been a loving mother to Joel.

She seemed different from Tabitha, but it was too soon for him to be sure. He found it difficult to believe that she could be so different from Tabitha and their father, especially since she hadn't bothered to inform Rafe about Joel.

Another surge of bitterness burned through him. He was in a position to pull off the ultimate revenge with the Livingstones. He could take Joel away and they would never see him again. Ultimate revenge was a gratifying prospect, but selfish. He had a son to think about now. The knowledge blew him away every time he thought of it.

Nicole could be useful. An image of her slid across his mind. She certainly wasn't his usual type. She wasn't the least bit flashy and kept her sensuality under wraps. Something about the woman made him curious in a sexual way. He suspected that when she let loose, she could be explosive. It would take the right man to light her fuse. In other circumstances, he would give in to his curiosity, but something far more important was at stake at the moment. His son.

The following evening, after dinner and a bath for Joel, Nicole helped her nephew into his footed pajamas and sat beside him in his little bed. "Which book do you want me to read tonight?" she asked.

Her heart squeezed tight as he lifted four books with a hopeful expression on his sweet face. He may be her nephew by blood, but in her heart, he was her son. And she'd made sure of that through the courts.

"Four?" she said. "I thought I was just going to read two tonight."

"But I like all of these," he said, looking at the books. The job of narrowing down his choices clearly put him at a loss.

She sighed. "Okay, but just this once," she said, knowing she wouldn't be able to hold the line when he asked her tomorrow night. She suspected she enjoyed these precious moments with him even more than he did.

He plopped into her lap and opened the first book about a giant strawberry and the mouse who wanted to eat it.

In the back of her mind, she wondered whether she would hear anything else from Rafe Medici. Encouraged that he hadn't contacted her last night or today, she relaxed just a smidgeon. His intensity had frightened her so much that she'd almost given in to her fear and taken Joel out of the country.

Since Tabitha had died when he was just six months old, Joel viewed Nicole as his mother. He turned to her when he was sick or hurt. He chattered with her, smiled and laughed, and lifted his arms for hugs.

The strong attachment claimed Nicole the day he was born. The delivery had been difficult and Tabitha had wanted her sister by her side. Tabitha developed an infection in the hospital and the next six months had been a roller-coaster ride for everyone involved. Nicole had taken extra time off from work to care for both Tabitha and Joel.

Tabitha had grown impatient with her doctor's warnings and often hadn't taken her medicine properly. She'd insisted on going out partying at night while Nicole cared for Joel.

One night she'd collapsed and was rushed to the hospital. The infection had taken over her body and she'd died within a week.

Devastated and in shock, Nicole had secured legal custody of Joel per Tabitha's instructions. Although her father had invited her and Joel to live with him, she'd turned him down. Nicole refused to subject Joel to her father's unpredictable temper.

The threat of Rafe Medici continued to buzz in the back of her mind like a fly bouncing against a window, but Nicole cuddled Joel against her and read the second book, and the third. Halfway through the fourth story, Joel's little body sagged against her, his chest rising and falling in slow even breaths.

Nicole smiled. He'd fallen asleep. She gently shifted him off of her, and he burrowed into his covers, but his eyes remained closed. She kissed his forehead and turned out the dinosaur lamp beside his bed and left his room.

Returning to her den, silence settled around her like a cloak. In the beginning, after Tabitha had just died, she'd had to talk herself down from panic at the enormous job she faced of raising her sister's child. Was she up for it? There was no choice, she'd realized. She would have to muddle through.

After teething, chicken pox and potty training, she didn't question herself as much. Joel was a happy, healthy little boy.

Now the silence just underlined the fact that she was alone. She used her remote to turn her sound system on low volume and skipped through the selections until she landed on a collection of mindless, but cheerful pop music. As she sipped the glass of water she'd left by the couch, habit made her reach for unfinished paperwork for her job.

After Joel went to bed at night, Nicole was aware of how alone she truly was. Her mother lived on the other side of the world. She couldn't trust her father.

Thank goodness for her cousin Julia. Julia frequently scolded her to go out more often, but Nicole found it difficult to leave Joel in the evenings. As for a man, well, Tabitha had been the natural man magnet. The man Nicole had been seeing just before Tabitha died hadn't been interested in taking on a ready-made family. When the time was right, maybe a man would come into her life. An average man who wasn't an egomaniac or obsessed with success. Someday perhaps, but not today.

She forced her attention to her work to distract herself. A half hour passed, and a knock sounded at her front door. She noticed the time, 8:30 p.m. and cautiously rose. Glancing through the peephole, Nicole felt her stomach clench. Her worst nightmare was standing on her front porch.

Two

Nicole considered not opening the door, but she didn't want Rafe Medici to continue ringing her doorbell, perhaps awakening Joel. Taking a quick shallow breath, she whisked the door open and met his gaze in silence, mentally girding herself for the battle she knew she faced.

"Joel is my son," he said in a rock-hard voice.

"Joel is mine, legally and in every other way that counts," she immediately responded. Keeping her voice cool wasn't difficult since her blood felt like ice.

"Tabitha was his mother," he said, his lips moving in a bitter smile. "I'm not surprised she didn't want me to know since she felt I was good enough for playing, but not for staying."

"Tabitha made her wishes clear in her will," Nicole said. "She knew Joel needed a loving, nurturing and stable home environment."

"Joel deserves to know his father," Rafe said, anger glinting in his gaze. "He's been deprived of that for almost four years."

"I can assure you that Joel hasn't suffered under my care. He is my top priority."

"That doesn't change the fact that he needs a father, too." Rafe looked past her. "Are we going to continue to discuss this on the front porch, or are you going to let me in?"

Reluctantly, she stepped aside. She couldn't help noticing how his tall, muscular body filled the small foyer. "If you wake up my son," she said, "I won't hesitate to call the authorities to have you removed from my home."

He gave her an odd look. "I rarely find it necessary to raise my voice," he said in a tone that oozed solid, quiet power.

Her thoughts immediately went in two different directions. With that kind of confidence, he wouldn't need to rant and rave like her father had. Perhaps he accomplished whatever he wanted through a single quelling glance. She looked at his powerful hands and her stomach dipped in fear. *Unless he used his fists.*

Tabitha had never said he'd actually hit her, but she'd called him the brawny, bully type. An unsophisticated, but initially charming man she'd apparently underestimated.

"It's time for me to meet my son," he said.

Her heart jumped in apprehension. "I don't want Joel's life disrupted. He's happy and secure. Meeting you would confuse him. Besides, it's clear you don't know anything about kids. He's been in bed for an hour."

"At some point, he'll realize he has a father. The later I wait, the more he and I will regret the loss of time. I have legal rights. If I need to pursue things that way, I will."

Nicole jerked her head around to meet his gaze. "Don't

you dare threaten me. What do you have to offer him? Where do you live? On some kind of playboy yacht? What kind of life is that for a child?"

Rafe's mouth tightened. "I'm willing to make adjustments for my son. He should be living with me. I can hire help."

Her blood boiled at the very thought. "Hire help? Why, how fatherly! I can't believe you want a real relationship with Joel. You just want control, just like Tabitha said."

Rafe stared at her and she realized she'd revealed too much. He rested his hands over his slim hips, his gaze taking her in, assessing her from head to toe. "What did Tabitha tell you about me?"

Her nerves jumping, she shrugged and stepped backward. "She said you frightened her. The two of you met at a club in Miami and had an affair that lasted a few months. She initially found you handsome and charming, although you seemed rougher around the edges than her usual boyfriends. Toward the end of the relationship, you became someone who wanted control of her." She stopped short of telling him that Rafe had reminded her too much of their father.

Rafe inhaled, his nostrils flaring slightly. His demeanor appeared calm, but his eyes glinted with emotion. "So you took her impression of me as gospel," he said. "Without ever meeting me."

Nicole blinked. "Why shouldn't I believe her? She was my sister."

"Then you also know she wasn't perfect," he pointed out.

"No one is perfect."

"Some people are more capable of fabricating lies than others," he said.

"If you're insinuating that Tabitha would lie about something this important—"

"Are you saying she never lied about other important things?" he asked.

She opened her mouth to protest, but faltered a half beat. "Nothing this important."

"You don't know me," he said. "You've made judgments about me based on one flighty woman's opinion. Are you as flighty as she was?"

"No," she impulsively responded, and wished she could take back the words. Sentence by sentence, he seemed to be defeating her stance. She had to protect Joel. "I won't let you make a mockery of my sister—the mother of Joel. Tabitha had her flaws, but everyone does. She loved life and she ended up practically giving her life when she gave birth to Joel. You need to leave."

She saw him tamp down a flicker of impatience that seemed to ooze from every pore. "I have rights, Nicole. I'm Joel's father. What if I'm not the man Tabitha said I am? How are you going to explain that to him when he starts asking where his father is?"

She felt the deepest, smallest sliver of doubt and tried to brush it aside, but it was like a small rock in her shoe. "I have to protect him."

"I'll give you one night to explain who I am. Day after tomorrow, I'm coming back to meet my son."

Panic rushed through her. "It's too soon."

"It's reasonable," he said, his tone final.

The next day, Nicole visited her cousin, Julia. She told her cousin about Rafe after Julia put her two-month-old daughter down for a post-feeding nap.

"Your best bet is to cooperate," Julia said, as she sank on to the leather couch and patted Nicole on the arm.

Nicole bit her lip. "There must be something I can do."

Julia, dressed in a sweatshirt and yoga pants, was practical in nearly every area of her life. It was why law was such a good fit. "There are lots of things you can do, sweetie, but they'll cost a ton of money and set up a huge amount of resentment between Joel's father and you. Are you sure you want to go down that road?"

Nicole sighed. "But what if he's a horrible father? What if he's—" She almost couldn't bring herself to say the word aloud. "Abusive," she whispered.

Julia sighed. "Then that's a different story." She lifted her mug of herbal tea and took a sip. "Do you have reason to believe he's abusive? What did Tabitha tell you?"

"She said he was a bully and that he reminded her of our father."

Julia gave a slow nod. She knew the dark, inner workings of Nicole's family. "I can see why that would alarm you."

"Alarm is a mild term."

Her cousin paused for a thoughtful moment. "I know you and Tabitha were close, but even you knew that she was prone to exaggeration."

"Yes, but about something this important?"

"I'm not taking this man's side, but I could see Tabitha calling someone a bully if they didn't let her have her way."

"I suppose so," Nicole said reluctantly.

"Look, I'm not suggesting you hand over Joel without finding out more about this man—"

"I would *never* give Joel up," Nicole said, her voice cracking with emotion.

Julia put her arm around Nicole's shoulders. "One thing you may want to consider is what does this man have to gain by claiming his rights to Joel? You've described him as a wealthy, successful playboy. He doesn't need any money that Tabitha may have left for Joel. Plenty of men would run screaming in the opposite direction. Particularly the kind of man you describe."

Nicole bit her lip again, remembering what Rafe had said about losing his father at a young age. A burst of sympathy squeezed past her defenses. What if the man wasn't the ogre Tabitha had described?

"As hard as it seems, my best advice is for you to get to know this man as much as you can. He *is* Joel's father. In this situation, he's holding all the cards. If he wanted to, he could take Joel away from you tomorrow and at best, the only thing you could do would be to delay it."

At 5:30 p.m., Rafe strode up the sidewalk to the well-kept two-story home belonging to Nicole Livingstone. He carried pizza and some cupcakes he'd picked up from a grocery store. Armed with information he'd gleaned from his attorney and his private investigator, he knocked on the front door.

In the last three days, Rafe had covered the gamut of emotions ranging from fury at Tabitha for concealing his son's existence from him to an aching sense of loss. Now, his focus was pure and simple. He would be a father to his son, and nothing would get in his way.

The door opened, and Nicole looked at him, her gaze filled with wariness. She took a breath, an audible breath, as if she were preparing herself for battle, and glanced at the pizza. A hint of a wry smile played over her lush mouth. "Excellent guess," she said. "Joel loves pizza."

"Pepperoni okay?" he asked, curious what had made her soften.

"Depends on his mood. He'll either pull them off and eat them or leave them on his plate."

"I also brought a few cupcakes," he said, referring to the contents in the plastic bag.

A doubtful expression crossed her face. "That much sugar at bedtime can be deadly."

"Just one. If you think about it, I've missed four birthdays."

Her gaze met his and clung for a surprising second. He saw a flash of empathy and the slightest drop of regret. He drank it in like water for a man dying of thirst. His private investigator had filled in a lot of gaps about Nicole. Her education—double master's degrees in medical administration and sociology; her job—health services coordinator for disabled veterans; her financial rating—superb; her love life—limited; her devotion to Joel—infinite. Despite the fact that Nicole was clearly the more reserved twin, the woman had a heart. That would work in his favor.

"You can forget about him eating four cupcakes in one evening," she said with defiance in her eyes.

"That's good. I planned to eat at least one myself."

Her lips twitched again then her face turned serious. "Come inside. Take it slow and don't talk about the future."

"Why not?"

"Because we haven't figured that out yet. Just knowing he has a father is enough for Joel to handle right now."

"Are you speaking for Joel or yourself?" Rafe challenged.

Irritation prickled through her. "You can't believe that you know more about what's best for Joel than I do."

"I know I'm his father. That's enough."

She clenched her jaw. "I am asking you not to discuss future plans with him."

"I intend to make it clear to Joel that he can count on

me being in his present and future," Rafe conceded. "That's all I can promise you for tonight."

She took a quick breath. "It's enough that you exist and you're here. Trust me, you're overwhelming enough," she said and turned away. "I'll get him."

Rafe suddenly felt a rush of excitement. Joel. His son would be walking into his life within seconds.

A little boy with short, curly brown hair and blazing blue eyes came toward him and studied him. "Mom says you're my father."

"Yes, I am," Rafe said.

Joel glanced at the box in Rafe's hands. "You have pizza," he said.

Rafe chuckled. "Yes, I do."

"I'm hungry."

"Then we should eat."

It was that simple. Within minutes, Nicole, Joel and Rafe were eating pizza. Tonight Joel was good with pepperoni and ate the slices after he plucked them from the pizza.

"What are your top three favorite things to do?" Rafe asked his son, fascinated by the young child that bore such a striking resemblance to him.

"Wii, reading stories and animals," Joel said before he took a big bite of pizza.

"What kind of stories?" Rafe asked, hungry for more information about his son.

"I like the strawberry story," Joel said, taking another big bite of pizza. "It has a mouse and a bear in it."

Rafe nodded. "I haven't read that one. I'll have to check it out."

"You can read mine," Joel said. "But you have to give it back cuz it's my favorite."

"Okay," Rafe said and smiled. "Thank you."

After dinner and a cupcake, Rafe played Wii with Joel. Throughout the evening, he felt Nicole studying him. He suspected he was being graded. He didn't really care what her opinion was, but he also knew that she could make it easier for Joel to adjust to having him as a father. If she fought him, he would still win, but it would be messy.

She was far different from the Tabitha he remembered. Tabitha had chattered a mile a minute and flaunted her body. Nicole appeared to think before she spoke. She wore a pair of jeans that weren't too tight, but still faithfully followed the curves of her hips and her long legs. Her pink cashmere sweater gave more of an impression of quiet femininity than va-va-voom.

He wondered if she ever cut loose. He wondered what it would take to arouse passion in that cautious gaze.

"Time for bath and bed," Nicole said.

"Oh, Mom," Joel protested. "I want to play some more Wii. He's a lot better than you are."

Rafe chuckled then coughed to cover it.

Nicole threw him a sideways glance of amusement.

"I'll come back and we can play again," Rafe said to his son.

Joel studied him. "You promise?"

Rafe's chest tightened with some emotion he couldn't name. "I promise."

"Okay," he said and Nicole sent him upstairs to his bedroom.

She led Rafe to the door. "Thank you for not pushing."

"That was just for tonight," he said and turned to look at her. "I'd like to get together with you sometime tomorrow. There are things we need to discuss without Joel."

To his surprise, she nodded. "I agree. I have several appointments in the morning, but I should be free by twelve-thirty."

"We can meet for lunch at one of my brother's restaurants. Peachtree Grill okay?"

"That will work."

Still all business, he thought, and made a split-second decision to remind her that he was a man and she was a woman. He took her hand in his and rubbed his thumb against the soft underside of her wrist. "Thanks for working with me on this."

Surprise and awareness flashed through her eyes. "You're, uh, welcome," she said and he removed his hand just before she would have.

He watched her rub her hand over her wrist as if it burned and felt a jab of satisfaction. The lady wasn't as cool as she pretended.

Nicole felt her pulse pick up as she killed her engine just outside the restaurant where she was to meet Rafe. She took a deep breath, telling herself that she was reacting to the threat he represented, not his masculine appeal.

So he'd done well with Joel last night. That hadn't been much of a test. A couple hours, she scoffed. That was nothing.

Grabbing her purse, she rose from the car and straightened her wool jacket, then walked toward the restaurant. A hostess wearing a short black dress and boots greeted her just inside the door.

"I'm here to meet Rafe Medici," she said noticing that the restaurant appeared to be nearly full.

The hostess shot her a smile as she guided her around

the corner. "Lucky girl. Come this way. Oh, look, the servers are swarming the poor guy."

Nicole glanced up and saw three women dressed in short skirts and white blouses standing in front of the wooden booth where Rafe sat.

The hostess cleared her throat loudly. "Excuse me. Here's Mr. Medici's lunch date."

Nicole wanted to correct the hostess. This wasn't a date—it was more of an inquisition. All three female servers turned to stare at Nicole in envy.

"Enjoy your meal," the hostess said and two of the servers left with her.

Rafe stood and slid his hand over hers for a sizzling instant. "Good to see you. What would you like to drink?"

"Coffee is fine," she said, feeling her heart bump at the way he looked at her. She forced her gaze away from his as she sat on the leather bench.

"Cream?" the lone remaining server asked.

"No, thank you. I'll take it black." Mentally girding herself, she looked up at him and couldn't help noticing how handsome he was. Heaven help her if Joel turned out this good-looking. She would be beating the girls off with a stick. It wasn't just Rafe's dark hair, attractive features and killer body that would weaken a woman's defenses. It was the liveliness in his eyes and his expressive mouth. His sheer attentiveness would boggle most women. She needed to make sure she didn't fall into that already overflowing group.

"How was your morning?" he asked, taking a sip of his coffee.

"Productive," she said, surprised he would be remotely interested. "I visited three clients and coordinated some additional services for one of them. Also received a referral."

"I've heard you're well liked by your clients and that the medical community considers you a bit of a bulldog, but still respects you."

"And where did you hear that?" she asked as her coffee was served.

"From a private investigator." He shrugged. "Don't waste your energy on outrage. You wouldn't talk to me, so I had to find out for myself. Wouldn't you have done the same if the roles had been reversed?"

The idea of having someone snoop into her business irritated her. "Would you say he's good at what he does?"

"Very," he said. "Why do you ask?"

"Maybe I can hire him to give me information about you."

Rafe met her gaze and she saw a flash of challenge in his eyes. Then he laughed and leaned back in his seat. "Go right ahead, but I can save you the money. Ask me anything. I'm yours for the next hour."

Three

Nicole wondered how many women had ripped off their clothes at the sight of his wicked smile. She could easily understand why Tabitha had been seduced by him. He possessed an electric appeal. The same way a bug zapper seduced mosquitoes and zapped them to death.

"Tell me about your family," she said after they'd placed their orders with the server.

He paused and his expression turned thoughtful. "As I told you, my father died when I was young. It was a train accident. One of my brothers died at the same time." She watched the grief cut through his eyes and felt a stab in her heart. "My mother couldn't handle us alone, so my brothers and I were placed in foster homes," his hand clenching into a fist. "Our world was blown apart."

Despite her huge doubts about Rafe's ability to be a

good father to Joel, his story tugged at something inside her. "That must have been difficult."

"It was, but a lot of things in life can be difficult. I was much luckier with my foster parents than my older brother was. He emancipated himself as a minor before he graduated from high school."

"Wow," she said, thinking of how insulated her boarding-school upbringing was in comparison. "What is he doing now?"

"Running an obscenely successful company with a few sidelines when it suits him. He just got married." A smile played over his lips. "He would do anything for her and she would do anything for him." A glint of envy crossed his face so quickly she wondered if she imagined it. "Not everyone is that lucky. He deserves it. I can afford to be generous. I finally beat him at pool," he joked.

"Sounds like an interesting family," she said, feeling a teensy bit envious at the camaraderie she heard in his voice.

"I'm betting it's worlds apart from yours," he said.

"Mine was—" She paused. "Is different from yours, that's for sure."

"In what way?" he asked.

The server brought the food and set it on the table. "Tabitha and I were sent off to boarding school by the time we were eight. I liked the structure more than Tabitha did." Nicole shook her head, laughing at a chain of memories that ran through her mind. "She was so wild. She would have gotten kicked out if I hadn't—" She broke off, even now respecting their vow of secrecy.

"If you hadn't?" he asked.

"Old news," she said, lifting her hand and dismissing his question.

"Your personality seems very different from hers," he said. "You look similar, though her hair was lighter, wasn't it?"

"She was a blonde in her heart. She lit up a room when she walked into it," Nicole said.

"And you?"

"After we grew up, I didn't usually walk into the same rooms she did. I was studying for my master's degree, working as a teaching assistant."

"Did you ever envy her?"

"Sometimes," she said, remembering the awesome experience of when Tabitha had given birth to Joel. Nicole had wished for the same, but she'd never let anyone get that close. "On the other hand, being the life of the party looks like a lot of work. Maybe it comes natural to some people. Like you?"

He lifted a dark brow. "I wasn't the life of the party. I was more interested in surviving. People will do lots of things to survive."

"Never thought of it that way," she said, pushing her salad around her plate and remembering how Tabitha had worked her way around her father in a way Nicole had never managed.

"Your mother is in France, right?" Rafe asked.

"More from my dossier?"

He gave her an unapologetic smile.

"Yes, she lives in France with a younger man and alimony from my father."

"Do you ever see her?"

"Not often. She's busy living the life she missed when she was married to my father."

"And your father?"

"We're not close," she said, averting her gaze. There was

too much bad blackness in that relationship. "I see him about once every couple of months."

"I would think he'd be interested in an heir for his business. A grandson would be a huge ego boost."

"I suppose the idea of a grandson is a huge ego boost. He definitely missed having a son, but my father has his priorities. I have mine. He's expanded his business more in the international market, so that keeps him out of town more." When Tabitha had died, her father had argued vehemently with her that *he* should be Joel's guardian instead of Nicole. Her second-best defense had been that he was out of town so frequently. Her number-one defense, however, had created an ugly tension between them.

"Who's your backup for Joel?"

She didn't like the turn of the conversation. "I have a cousin with a baby. We're very close. She's there for me when I need her, but I've been able to handle most of my parental responsibilities myself. I've chosen the best preschool and I've arranged my job so that I have flexibility if I need to take a day off."

"Superhero," he said.

"No," she said. "Just the best substitute mom I can be."

"He calls you Mom."

Her heart contracted at the reminder. "I had a hard time with that in the beginning, but then I realized that Joel needed to feel like he had a mom. I was it."

"What else do you want to know about me?" he asked.

She gave a short laugh and smiled. "Everything. Just everything. What's your attitude toward corporal punishment?"

"The death penalty?" he asked, crinkling his eyes in his confusion.

"No. Spanking children."

"Oh," he said, realization crossing his face. "I was spanked as a child, but Lord, there's got to be a better way. Time out, no cupcakes, no Wii. Something's gotta work. What do you think?"

Surprised that he'd turned the question on her, she paused a half beat. "All of those," she said. "I've been fortunate with Joel. He responds well to other methods. If there's a problem area, I try to work up a reward system. We've used star stickers before," she said, smiling.

"Star stickers," he said. "I got them when I read a book, cleaned the commode, mopped the floor or made the honor roll."

"How often did you make the honor roll?" she asked, curious.

"Not as often as you did, I bet," he said. "I played football."

"Ah, a jock," she said, the words coming out before she could edit them.

"And you were a nerd," he said. "A hot nerd."

"Just a nerd," she said.

"You wouldn't have looked twice at a football-playing, low-class guy like me," he teased.

She suspected she would have secretly lusted after him. "Oh, I don't know. I always envied others with athletic skills."

He gave a rough laugh that skittered down her nerve endings. "What kind of boys did you torment during high school?"

"None," she said, then remembered the geeky guy from a neighboring boys' school that had seemed to have a crush on her. "Okay, maybe one or two. I left most of that for Tabitha. She came out of the womb ready to seduce the world."

"What about you?"

"I came out shy and tentative, a little awkward. I needed to think things over."

"And now? Where is the man in your life?" he probed.

"The man in my life is Joel," she said in a deliberately cool voice. "For the sake of my son, my love life and my party life can wait. Can yours?"

He met her gaze. "Is that what you're afraid of? My wild lifestyle?"

She shrugged. "I have to think about what's best for Joel."

"I'd be lying if I told you I was a monk or a saint, but I didn't become successful by partying every night. Contrary to your dubious opinion of me, I've worked damn hard."

Nicole inwardly winced. She'd gone too far. "I didn't mean to suggest that you—"

"And if you're worried about women—"

"I—"

"My tastes have changed in the last five years. I know better than to let a spoiled little heiress wrap me around her finger and squeeze my guts out."

Nicole felt the punch of his confession in her stomach. So he had genuinely cared for Tabitha. Confusion raced through her. Tabitha had conveyed that Rafe had merely viewed her as a plaything—his plaything to control. She struggled with his description of her sister.

"I think it would be a good idea for you to hire that P.I. Hell, I'll pay for it. You can hire a different one if you're afraid he'll be biased."

She wondered if he was daring her. What he didn't understand was that she would do anything to protect Joel. "I suspect that you would only hire the best, so I'll take your recommendation. But I'll pay for it." She glanced at her watch. "I should go. Thank you for your time and lunch," she said, looking at the plate of food she'd barely touched. Nerves had chased away her appetite.

"I'll walk you out," he said, rising as she did.

"It's not necessary," she said. "I'm parked just across the street."

She began to pull on her jacket and he reached over to assist her. The considerate gesture bothered her. One more little bit of evidence that perhaps he wasn't a monster after all. Was it possible that Tabitha would have lied to her?

Rafe escorted her through the crowded restaurant. He was the kind of man to draw glances. His confidence and charm were magnetic. He opened the door and chuckled under his breath.

She shot him a questioning look.

"I'm not used to winter. I left my jacket in my brother's office. We'll probably trade some trash talk over the weather."

"Like what?" she asked, curious.

"He'll call me a lightweight. I'll tell him he's just jealous because he doesn't live in the tropics in winter."

She couldn't resist a smile. "Please tell him he's done a great job with this restaurant."

"Despite the fact that you hardly ate any of your meal," he said.

"It would have been nice if you hadn't commented on that," she said, feeling self-conscious because she wanted to project complete confidence.

"There's nice and there's stupid. Sometimes you have to choose one or the other. But I'll let you tell my brother what you think of his place. You'll meet him. You and I are just getting started," he said.

The expression in his dark eyes bordered on sensual, but that couldn't be possible, Nicole thought. Not in their situation. He was just a humongous flirt. He probably flirted with ninety-year-old women. Perhaps that was part of his appeal.

"Good-bye for now, then," she said and stepped into her car, wishing he didn't affect her the way he did. He pushed the door closed and stepped backward with a wave. Nicole shored up her defenses as she pulled away. She wouldn't be deceived by his charm. As soon as she got home, she would call that investigator and ask for a full report on Rafe Medici.

She didn't trust him. If he couldn't be a good father to Joel, she might have to do the unthinkable. She might have to take Joel and flee from the country. Leaving the States would give her at least a shot at keeping Joel safe if Rafe turned out to be abusive. It would be far easier for her and Joel to disappear in a foreign country. The prospect terrified her. Nicole had always been a rule follower, but there was too much at stake now. After she put Joel to bed tonight, she would put together a contingency plan for how to get away from Rafe Medici.

Even though it was too damn cold, Rafe watched Nicole as she drove away. She was a peculiar mix, way too strait laced for his taste. But when she smiled, it was genuine, and warmth radiated from her. When she gave in to that husky little laugh, the sound grabbed at his gut. She was the kind of woman a man had to earn. Not so much because she counted on her beauty and wiles. She could have if she wanted to. She was certainly beautiful. No, the reason a guy would have to earn her attention was because she didn't give it away easily.

Rafe worked from Michael's house the rest of the day. He should have been tired, but it took him a long time to fall asleep. He finally drifted off to a restless sleep.

Flames surrounded him, the sound of screams stabbed at him. He watched his father's face stretch into a grimace of pain.

Rafe heard his father shout.

The agony of the sound sent a bolt of terror through him. He saw his brother Leo screaming in fear. "Daddy, Daddy!"

Rafe ran toward his father and Leo, struggling to save them. Just as he grew close, a wall shot up between them. The wall was acrylic. He could see through it, but he couldn't get past it.

Beating against the wall, he watched his father and brother suffer as flames engulfed them.

"Let me," he yelled. "Let me..." His knuckles bled as he hammered his fists against the wall. "Dad...Leo..."

His father's face turned gray, the color of death. Leo's scream filled his brain. Rafe ran, desperate to save them both.

A cramp knotted his calf, jolting him awake. He swore under his breath, sitting upright in his bed, gasping for air. Sweat drenched his body. His heart pounded. He needed to get his father. He needed to save Leo.

Several seconds passed before he realized he'd been locked in a dream. The same dream he'd experienced since he'd been told that his father and Leo had died in the train accident. He'd spent so many nights wanting to fix it. To rescue his father and Leo. It had been too late, but he still wanted to save them.

He still had to try.

Sucking in a deep breath of air, he rose from his bed and paced from one end of his bedroom to the other. The wetness on his skin began to dry. It had been a dream, although years ago, some of it had been all too real. He couldn't have done anything about it when it had happened.

That tragic reality swept through him for the hundredth time. He couldn't do anything about it now, either, he thought, inhaling deeply.

Rafe thought of Joel and Nicole. He could do something about them, he thought. And he would. Nothing would stop him. He would never be helpless again.

Early the next morning he put together a plan.

His BlackBerry rang, interrupting his thoughts. He glanced at the caller ID.

"Maddie," he said to his assistant. "What's up?"

"I thought you should know that Mr. Argyros is in town and he's been asking for you more than once. I get the impression he may be looking to acquire."

"He's always worked with Livingstone in the past. He may just be trying to work another deal."

"True," she said.

He felt a familiar gnaw of hunger—the possibility of winning. "How long is he in town?"

"I don't know for sure, but I think he said something about three more days."

Rafe raked his hand through his hair and stifled a sigh. He was accustomed to making quick, difficult decisions. This one was a little more difficult than usual, but it didn't stop him. "Okay, I need you to find a house for me."

"A house?" his assistant echoed. "Wow. Did you have anything particular in mind?"

"I have a son. Changes need to be made. I'm bringing my son back to Miami with me."

A long, full silence followed. "A...son?" she whispered.

"Yeah. I'm bringing his—" He paused, narrowing his eyes. "Mother."

"Oh," she said.

"It's complicated."

"Sounds like it," she said.

"I'll give you more instructions tomorrow."

"We have to leave for Miami the day after tomorrow," Rafe said as he made an unexpected visit the following night.

Nicole gaped at him. "Excuse me?"

"It's business. I can't wait any longer and I won't leave Joel behind."

Nicole's stomach clenched. "Why not? Joel has been fine here with me."

"Joel's my son. I won't leave him behind. I'll never leave him behind again."

She saw his deadly determination and felt a chill shoot through her. "It's not that easy. Joel doesn't even know you. Do you have any idea how traumatic this will be for him to be jerked away from everything he knows?"

"Then come with him," he said.

Nicole blinked. She'd spent the previous evening making arrangements with the private investigator and making contingency plans to leave the country with Joel. "I don't know what to say," she said.

He shrugged. "If Joel is really your priority, it should be an easy decision."

"But I have a job."

"Take a leave of absence."

"You make it sound so easy."

"It is," he said, his eyes dark with determination and daring. "What's most important to you? Your security or Joel's?"

She took a shallow breath. "Joel's security is most important, of course. I just don't understand why this has to be done immediately. Why can't you take care of your business and then we can arrange for a getting-acquainted visit next month?"

He shook his head before she finished her suggestion. "Not next month. Now. My son is going to live under my roof. I'll be arranging for full custody. You can either help or get out of the way. I can get a court order by tomorrow morning."

"How am I supposed to make all these arrangements? Get everything packed?"

"Don't worry about packing. I can pay for everything you and Joel could need or want."

She shook her head. "You just don't understand. Security doesn't always come from money and things. It comes from people and familiarity."

"I'll be that person for Joel. My home will become that place for him, too." He paused three heartbeats. "Are you coming or not?"

"You've given me no choice."

"You're valuable to my son. I'll make sure you're well-rewarded financially."

Anger roared through her. "I don't want your money," she told him. "If I wanted money, I could turn to my father and play his game. Maybe you're no better than he is," she said, spitting out the words, giving him the ultimate insult.

Rafe shrugged. "You'll find out soon enough," he said. "My private jet will take us to Miami no later than Thursday morning. Let me know what you need, but be ready."

"Why do you want him?" she demanded. "It's not as if you'll pay any attention to him. It's not as if he's suffering without you. Why must you have him with you when he's clearly thriving without you?"

"He may be thriving now, but no one can know the

future. Not even you, I won't have my son go through what I did. I'll protect him with every cent of my fortune."

"A father is more than money and fortune," she said. She knew that more than most. "What is it going to take for you to realize that?"

"I have time to learn what I need to know about being Joel's father as long as he's with me, and that's going to start the day after tomorrow."

Fuming, fussing, full of fear, Nicole wrangled a leave of absence from her boss and began to pack. She needed to take Joel's favorite books and stuffed toys, and his favorite blanket, the photo collage of Tabitha and his baby-picture scrapbook.

Terrified at the prospect of losing him, she put herself on fast-forward. She had a job to do. She needed to focus on that, not her fear. In the back of her mind, she held on to her plan of taking Joel and fleeing from the country. *If Rafe was a bad father.*

As long as she worked with him, she was buying time before he took legal action. Right now, she still possessed Joel's passport and the ability to leave the country.

Nicole worked through the day and described the trip to Miami as an adventure when she picked up Joel from nursery school. "You'll get to spend some time at the ocean."

"I can swim?" Joel asked, getting excited. "Will I use my water wings?"

She nodded as she gripped the steering wheel. "Or a life jacket. You'll get to go on a big boat, too. Rafe owns a lot of big boats."

"Like Grandfather?" Joel asked, referring to Nicole's father.

Her chest tightened. "In a way," she said, praying that Rafe wasn't like her father. "It's warmer there than it is here," she said. "You won't have to wear a coat."

A long silence followed. "Will you go with me?" Joel asked in a worried voice.

"Of course, sweetie."

"Will you stay with me?"

Her heart twisted. "I'll always make sure you're safe. You're the most important thing in the world to me."

Joel let out a big breath. "Will you swim with me?"

Nicole smiled. "Sure."

"Can I take my favorite book?"

"It's already packed," she said. "You can check my list and tell me if we need to add something else. Okay?"

"Okay," he said.

Nicole glanced at him and spotted a smile on his face. His expression tugged at her.

"I get to go to the beach," he said.

Rafe issued a few last-minute instructions to his assistant. He glanced up and saw Nicole holding Joel's hand as they walked toward him. He exhaled in relief, surprising himself with the emotion. Part of him had wondered if Nicole would find a way to bail at the last moment.

Despite the cool expression on her face, something about the woman assured him. He wasn't sure if it was her protectiveness of his son, her willingness to challenge him, her mysterious beauty, or a combination of all three that got to him.

He shouldn't trust Nicole one inch. How could he? She was Tabitha's twin. Nicole had to share some similarities with the woman who'd betrayed him. With all the time they'd spent together in the womb and growing up together, it would have been a miracle if at least a few of Tabitha's faults hadn't rubbed off on Nicole. Those flaws would show up soon enough, he reminded himself. At the moment, she was useful to him.

He looked at his son and lifted his hand for a fist bump. Joel lifted his small fist, too. "Do Mom," he said.

Surprise crossed Nicole's face. "That's okay, honey," she said.

"No," Rafe said, unable to resist the urge to challenge her, and lifted her hand to meet his. "Ready to go?"

"Do you want me to answer that question honestly?" she asked, her eyes revealing a beguiling combination of vulnerability and defiance.

He glanced at the luggage the chauffeur had brought behind. "Looks like you did pretty well to me."

"I had no choice," she said.

"You can relax now. You're in good hands," he told her and covered her hand with his. He saw a flicker of awareness race through her eyes. He felt the same quickening inside him.

"We'll see," she said and the doubt in her voice raised his hackles. After all he had accomplished, he wasn't accustomed to having anyone question his abilities. Besides Tabitha, no woman had expressed anything but confidence in him. Soon enough, Nicole would see that he could handle anything thrown at him and excel at it. This would be no different.

Four

Nicole helped Joel get settled into his seat beside the window. Her little boy was bursting with excitement at the prospect of his first flight, his gaze glued to the view from the sky as they took off. Sinking into her own butter-soft leather seat of Rafe's private luxury jet, Nicole accepted the juice and coffee offered by the staff and felt her muscles soften.

For the moment, both men in her life were occupied—Rafe with work, Joel with the window. Luxury surrounded her. The sensation wasn't entirely new. She'd been raised in luxury, but learned to live without since she'd gone to college. Independence from her father had been far more important to her than all the things his money could buy. She would need to make sure she didn't grow accustomed to the ease Rafe's wealth provided because she knew that ultimately she wouldn't be staying.

She offered Joel some orange juice, but he was too distracted by the flight to drink.

"Nicole," Rafe said in a low voice, drawing her attention to him. "Come here for a minute," he said pointing to the seat next to his.

She moved reluctantly, as if she were approaching a predatory animal. Like a panther, Rafe might be beautiful on the outside, but on the inside, she knew he could be ruthless.

"As soon as we touch down, a car will pick us up to take us to our new home. Then—"

"Your yacht?" she asked.

"No, I told my assistant to find a house for us. If we don't like it, we can choose something else," he said. "Feel free to call her with any questions when I'm not available. I'll give you her contact info. I've arranged to have some of my staff from the yacht transfer to the house for convenience's sake. The chef can prepare anything—from sushi to gourmet French and Italian food."

"But can he make a grilled-cheese sandwich?" she couldn't resist asking.

He paused a half beat and shot her a ghost of a smile. "Very good," he said. "We can work on the legal transfer of his guardianship in the next couple of—"

She felt her heart plunge to her feet. "Excuse me? Legal transfer?" She balled her fingers into tight fists.

He nodded as he studied her. "Of course," he said. "It has to be done sometime. There's no need to wait. I'm Joel's father. I will have custody."

She swallowed over the lump in her throat. "My understanding is that the court may want to appoint someone to aid in the transition," she said.

"That will be you," he said. "It would be stupid for it to

be anyone else. You know Joel best. There's no need to traumatize him."

She felt a sliver of relief. "Okay. There will also be visits from social services."

Irritation crossed his features. "It's just a formality."

"They'll want to make sure you're a fit parent."

He narrowed his eyes. "My personal experience with social services is that they are too overworked to spend much time on cases where a biological parent is able and willing to care for his child."

She lifted her finger to her lips when he raised his voice and glanced over her shoulder to check on Joel. His little face was still pressed against the window. "I didn't make the rules."

"I'm his biological father. That should be more than enough."

"Technically, you're still an unproven quantity when it comes to parenting. Social services will want to make sure you're taking care of him properly."

She could tell he was offended that anyone would dare question his right to parent Joel. He scowled. "I don't expect any interference."

While Rafe talked on his cell phone, the chauffeur drove the limo down a driveway lined with palm trees and bougainvillea to a large mansion with white columns on either side of the front door. It was huge even compared with the standards of Nicole's upbringing.

As the limo pulled to a stop, Rafe turned off his cell phone. His gaze met hers and she felt an odd sensation in her stomach. Hunger, it had to be hunger.

A half smile lifted his lips. "So, what do you think of

it?" he asked, lifting one of his hands in the direction of the house. "It has a pool, tennis courts, several whirlpools, big backyard for Joel…"

"Is this where you live?" Joel asked, his eyes rounded.

"Where *we* live," Rafe corrected.

The chauffeur opened the door to help Nicole out of the car. Rafe slid his hand to her back, and ushered her up the steps. Nicole felt a rush of discordant feelings. Could Joel be happy in this huge mansion? How would she ever be able to leave him here? "It's definitely different than our home in Atlanta."

"I wanted a place when you and Joel would be comfortable."

She felt a trickle of relief that he'd included her in the offhand explanation, but knew she couldn't count on that. "There will have to be strict rules about the pool," she said, her mind moving to safety concerns. "Perhaps even some kind of alarm system. I wouldn't be able to live with myself if anything happened to him," she said.

"Good point," he said. "I'll get Maddie to take care of that right away."

"Maddie?"

"My assistant. Here she is," he said, as a lovely young woman with short, sexy blond hair walked out the front door of the house toward them. She wore business capris, a stylish tank and blouse, and heels. She emanated an air of confidence.

"Hi, I'm Maddie. You must be Nicole," she said, extending her hand. "Your resemblance to your sister is incredible. The hair color and the clothes are different, but—"

"Did you know her?" Nicole asked.

"I was working part-time for Rafe when they were

involved. And little Joel is a doll," she added. "Spitting image of Rafe."

Joel's hand tightened around hers. "With Tabitha's eyes," Nicole felt compelled to add.

"Maddie, do you mind giving Nicole the tour while I make a few calls?" Rafe asked.

Maddie gave Rafe a blinding smile. "Not at all. I live to serve."

Nicole wondered if there was something more than business between the two, then reminded herself that it shouldn't matter to her.

Rafe slid his hand down Nicole's arm, short-circuiting her thoughts.

"I'll see you later."

Nicole resisted the urge to rub away the effect of his touch, forcing her attention to the house.

Maddie led her and Joel into the house through a foyer with a cool marble floor. They strolled through a kitchen, dining room, two downstairs dens, a library/game room with pool table, a master bedroom downstairs, and housekeeper's quarters. A patio and large pool stood just outside the back door. Beyond that, tennis courts and a large grassy yard.

"You must always have an adult with you before you go into the pool," Nicole said to Joel, bending down on her knee and looking into his eyes. "Always."

"What if you're not here?" he asked, his gaze straying to the tempting blue water.

"Then you wait until I am here," she said. "Promise me."

He met her gaze. "I promise."

Nicole brushed a kiss on his soft cheek. "Good boy."

"There will be other people who can swim with—"

"When he's older," Nicole said, cutting off the cute,

pert woman. "Sometimes you don't have second chances when it comes to safety."

Maddie shot her a slightly piqued expression. "There's more upstairs," Maddie muttered.

Maddie led the way past several more bedrooms and baths, along with a playroom where Joel immediately began exploring the many new toys. Even though the mansion needed more furniture before it would feel like a home, Nicole couldn't help being impressed with how much decorating progress had already been made.

"How did you do this so quickly?" Nicole asked.

Maddie laughed. "Rafe and I have been together so long. He can give me a few sentences," she said and snapped her fingers, "and I know exactly what he wants."

Nicole felt the little stab of a question again about their relationship. "Where will I sleep?"

"I thought I'd put you near Joel in this wing. Rafe will take the other wing."

"I don't think I saw that."

Maddie hesitated a half beat. "Oh, I guess I forgot. There's a master bedroom on each floor. The master on this floor is all the way down the hall and to the left. It includes a gym because Rafe is very big on working out. Now about the nanny—"

"Nanny," Nicole repeated, frowning. "I'm here Joel won't need a nanny."

Maddie hesitated again. "Perhaps not in the traditional sense. But you may find you'll need someone to take care of the driving and to give you breaks. I've already set up a meeting for Joel at a preschool based on what Rafe described to me."

"I'll need to visit before a final decision is made."

"Of course," Maddie said, but something about her voice bothered Nicole. She gave a smile that didn't quite reach her eyes. "It really is remarkable how similar the two of you looked. I almost feel as if I'm looking at a ghost."

"We were identical twins with very different personalities."

Maddie nodded. "Rafe and Tabitha were like oil and water. I knew it wasn't going to work from the beginning. Rafe doesn't need a pampered heiress. He needs more of an independent type."

Nicole felt a rush of protectiveness for her sister. "Tabitha may not have been perfect, but no one is. If it weren't for Tabitha, we wouldn't have Joel."

Impatience flashed through Maddie's eyes and her lips tightened. "You're right. Without Tabitha, there would be no Joel," she said, her tone laced with irritation. "Now tomorrow, I'll be sending over three na—" She broke off and corrected herself. "Three candidates to assist you with Joel. Choose which one you like best and then perhaps you can visit the preschool in the afternoon. I would have sent the assistants today, but Rafe insisted you and Joel needed a chance to relax." Maddie led the way down the stairs then pressed her card into Nicole's hand. "I know you're only staying here temporarily, but Rafe and I want to make sure you're as comfortable as possible. In his position he can get terribly busy, so if you need anything at all, please feel free to call me."

The proprietary tone in Maddie's voice rose again. It grated on Nicole, although she couldn't say why. "Thank you. Hopefully Joel and I will be able to manage on our own."

"Okay. I'll just have a word with Rafe before I leave. Good-bye now," Maddie said and turned away.

Nicole walked to the kitchen to get a bottle of water and

surveyed the contents of the refrigerator. Hearing footsteps behind her, she turned to find Rafe looking at her.

"Hungry?" he asked. "We have a housekeeper and chef. I'm sure they can whip up whatever you like."

"I was just looking to see what I could fix for Joel tonight."

He shook his head and closed the refrigerator door. "You're not preparing meals. You're supposed to help Joel adjust."

"That's part of making him adjust," she said. "I always cook at home."

"Tell the chef the time you want dinner and what you want. Would you like to take a shower, spend some time in the Jacuzzi?"

"I might have time for that. I'm not sure when I'll be able to pry Joel out of the playroom. He's fascinated by all the new toys. You need to be careful about spoiling him."

"I know, but I've got four years to make up for. Plus, I want him to be comfortable here."

"But will you be?" she asked. "Won't you miss living on the sea?"

"I'll be there every day." He shrugged. "Maybe I can take the three of us out for a weekend if I ever get caught up. Maddie gave you the rundown on the applicants for the nanny position, right?"

"Yes, and I told her that since I'll be here, Joel won't need a nanny."

He shook his head. "You've had to do this by yourself for a long time. You may not want to admit it, but I'm sure there have been times when being a single parent has been overwhelming. I want you to have all the help you need."

"Thank you," she said, still a little irked by the idea. "About Maddie," she said.

"She's amazing, isn't she? Most efficient woman I've ever met," he said.

She opened her mouth to ask the question that burned inside her, then thought better of it. "Very efficient."

"Take some time to relax." He nodded and put his hand on her arm. "You and I can talk more after dinner."

After Nicole finally got Joel settled in for the night, she wandered downstairs to join Rafe on the patio. He stood, staring into the distance, appearing lost in thought. She didn't know what to make of him. His strength appealed to her at the same time that it frightened her. Was he the kind of man to use his strength against those weaker than him?

She hesitated joining him, but he must have sensed her presence because he turned around. "Hi. Have a seat. I bet you're tired."

"Not too much," she said and sat down.

He pointed to the two glasses of wine on the table. "Have some wine."

"Thank you. It's been a long day."

He sat beside her. "Tomorrow will be easier."

Taking a sip of the red wine, she was not at all sure she agreed with him. "This is just the first day in a whole new world."

"It will be much easier for both you and Joel now. You won't have to worry about financial matters. You'll have assistance whenever you need it. I have to tell you I'm still surprised that you and Joel didn't live with your father."

Her stomach clenched. "My father can be controlling. With him it's his way or the highway. I've found it's better for me to go my own way."

"What about Tabitha?" he asked.

"Tabitha had a different relationship with our father. She was able to walk a fine line of charm with him and most of the time, it worked."

"When it didn't?" he asked.

"It wasn't pleasant," she said.

"Are you saying—"

"I'd rather not discuss my father, if you don't mind," she said and fought against that trapped feeling she so strongly associated with her father. She didn't have to discuss him, she reminded herself and rose.

"Let's walk," he said, superseding her desire to leave. He stood and took a sip of red wine, then led the way into the landscaped backyard, lit with soft floodlights and trees wrapped in minilights.

"It's beautiful," she said, the sound of crickets calming her.

"Nice," he agreed, shoving his hands into his pockets. "I'm used to the sound of the water lapping against the boat, the gentle movement of the yacht, the smell of salt air."

She glanced at him. "You sound like you're homesick."

"Maybe a little," he said. "The sea is cleansing. The rhythm of the waves is soothing. Even though I conduct business on my yacht, I can turn it all off if I want and just enjoy the ocean. No crowds, no rush. Instant getaway from it all."

Nicole couldn't help thinking how Tabitha had always wanted to be in the middle of the party. "How in the world did you ever get involved with my sister?" she couldn't help asking.

He chuckled again. "You have to admit she was a head snapper, seductive when she found something she wanted, charming."

She nodded reluctantly. "She was charming. But you seem deeper, smarter. How could you have fallen for her?"

"I was younger. She was everything I wasn't. Privileged. Pedigreed. Classy. I was a foster kid from the poor part of Philadelphia. She was a dream come true."

"And she was beautiful, wild and sexy," Nicole said.

"She was beautiful and alluring. Wild at times. Sexy, but not really sexual."

"Really?" Nicole said, unable to contain her curiosity, even though she knew this was a taboo topic. "I always got the impression she was a man-eater."

"Not in a sexual way," he said. "She was actually perfunctory about sex. Hot before, but not so much during."

Nicole gaped at him. She'd always thought that Tabitha made men crazy with her sexuality.

"You seem surprised," he said, his expression amused.

"I never knew—" She broke off. "I just heard what she said about herself and what other people said about her."

Meeting her gaze, he nodded. "I've learned that some women are hotter when they're teasing than when they deliver." He looked at her as if he wanted to find out if she fit into the first or second category.

Surprised at the rush of heat that suffused her, she took a quick, calming breath. "Tabitha talked about being a master of the tease."

"She was," he said. "That seemed to be all she wanted out of it. There's more to pleasure than teasing."

His dark gaze felt as if he penetrated all the way to her soul. She was acutely aware of the contrast between his masculinity and her femininity. The night seemed to close around them and curiosity trickled through her. It had been a long time since she'd felt curious about a man, since she'd felt desire. Why now? Why with him?

She should back away. Right this second, she told

herself, but her feet may as well have been lead weights. She held her breath as he stepped closer and lifted his hand, rubbing his fingers over a strand of her hair. "Soft," he said. "You could be a crazy-making contradiction."

Her heart hammering in her chest, she swallowed. "What do you mean?"

"Soft hair, soft skin, a voice that reminds me of good brandy. All that softness and a titanium backbone."

She couldn't help laughing at the wry tone when he'd described her backbone. "Ah, you're just used to being surrounded by yes men and yes women. The great Rafe Medici has spoken, so that's the way it goes."

"Ah, you think I'm great," he said and his lips lifted in a sensual smile that sent ripples all the way down her body.

"I'm sure you can find crowds of people who will tell you how great you are. You don't need another one," she said, wishing she could pull back, but his fingers on her hair kept her captive. Or was it the way he looked at her that prevented her from moving away.

"Sometimes one is more compelling than a crowd," he said and gently tugged her hair, drawing her closer to him.

"I've been curious about that mouth of yours since the first time I saw it, since the first time you blew me off. I'm betting you're a little curious about me. I think it's time we took care of our curiosity," he said in a such a low voice that she couldn't turn away.

He lowered his head and she should have backed away, should have at least turned her cheek or dipped her head, but she didn't. Although she would die before she confessed it, she was curious about Rafe Medici. Too curious.

It was just a kiss. Just one, she thought. Then never again. His mouth pressed against hers and she immediately felt dizzy. Closing her eyes, she inhaled the scent of his cologne, the promise of strength from his chest just inches from hers. The sensation of his mouth was both firm and sensually soft as he rubbed against her lips as if he was determined to savor her.

She instinctively parted her lips and he gave a low groan of sexy encouragement. Nicole felt a ripple of awareness in her most sensitive places. Yet, he only touched her lips.

Her heart rate picked up and a burgeoning need swelled inside her. *More.* She wanted to slide her breasts against him. She wanted to feel his arms around her. She wanted…

She could sense that he wanted more, too. He slid his tongue over the seam of her lips and she opened for him, giving in to her curiosity, in to the delicious, decadent sensations he generated in her.

He plunged his tongue deeper, as if tasting weren't enough. He wanted to devour. Her mind began to spin and she reached for his shoulders, trying to stabilize herself, but he slid his arms around her and drew her flush against the front of his hard body.

She felt his arousal and the craving inside her tightened like an overstretched rubber band. Breathless, but loath to pull away from him, she returned his kiss with a passion that surprised her.

Seconds later, he pulled back slightly, lifting his head. His eyes glittered with potent arousal. His nostrils flared slightly as he caught his own breath.

"I don't think one kiss is going to take care of our curiosity."

Five

Rational thought returned slowly. Nicole felt a hard smack of regret. Shaking her head, she backed away. "Oh, no. I can't believe—"

He put his hands on his hips and looked skyward. "Oh, tell me you're not going to play the innocent virgin who was taken advantage of by the bad, bad man."

She blinked at his description. "Well, I'd like to, but I'm not that innocent and it's not like you forced me." She bit her lip, trying to pull herself together. "Combination of wine and a long day," she said, turning toward the house. "I like that explanation much better."

"Explanation or excuse?" he asked as he walked beside her, one stride of his for every two of hers.

"Either is fine with me. I'm sorry for giving you the wrong impression."

He stepped in front of her just before she reached the door. "The word is teasing," he said. "Must run in the family."

"I said I'm sorry." She swallowed. "We shouldn't be doing this. I need to keep a clear head about Joel. He's my first priority."

"We have Joel in common," he said. "You and I are already entangled."

How could she possibly maintain the cautious perspective she needed if they became lovers? What about the warnings Tabitha had made? "There's also your history with my sister."

"And that's been over for more than four years."

Frustration and apprehension skittered through her like jabbing needles. "Why me?" she demanded. "You could have any woman you want. You probably *do* have any woman you want."

"I'm not sure if that was an insult or not," he said. "But have you ever considered that I'm intrigued by your combination of class and determination? You're naturally beautiful, but you don't flaunt it. Under the right conditions, I suspect you're a sweetheart. And now I know there's fire underneath. You know it, too. We both got hot when I kissed you. Do you really think you're going to be able to dismiss that?" He gave a short chuckle. "When you wake up in the morning, do you really think you're not going to feel that burn anymore?"

Deep down, she knew he was right. She also knew that being with him would be so wrong.

The only reason Nicole slept well that night was because she was exhausted. When she awakened in the morning, Joel was already back in the playroom. She hugged him tightly and learned he'd already eaten breakfast, but he was eager to play with all those new toys. The doorbell rang and the housekeeper, Carol, announced the arrival of the first *mother's helper* candidate.

Hours later, after intermittent breaks to check on Joel, Nicole had interviewed all three candidates. She still felt reluctant to choose one of the three applicants. It seemed to underscore her departure as Joel's primary caregiver.

Maddie called to ask what her decision was and Nicole told her she wanted to sleep on it. Maddie also informed her that Rafe probably wouldn't be home tonight. Yay, thought Nicole. By dinnertime, Joel was exhausted and needed to settle down. Nicole read two books to him and he fell asleep during the second book. She almost nodded off herself.

Giving a silent whisper of thanks that Rafe hadn't come home, she gave in to the temptation to take a dip in the Jacuzzi next to the pool. For just a few moments, she told herself. Then she would go to bed and sleep like a baby.

She pushed the button to turn on the jets and slid into the steamy, bubbling water with a sigh of appreciation. Since she'd stepped into the role of mothering, she'd pushed aside any kind of sensual pleasure so that she could care for Joel. He was more important than visits to the spa, more important than massages or facials, or even a long bath. She hadn't realized how much she'd missed a good soak, how rejuvenating it could be.

Rafe arrived to a quiet house. As he entered the foyer, he heard only the ticking of the grandfather clock he'd requested that Maddie purchase. The sound reminded him of a similar clock in the house his parents had rented in Philly.

A yawning edginess scraped across his nerves. He grabbed a bottle of water. He climbed the stairs to the second floor, checked on Joel as the boy slept peacefully. Rafe had missed the kid today. He walked into his master bedroom and prowled the large suite, glancing outside the floor-to-ceiling windows.

Spotting Nicole in the lit Jacuzzi next to the pool, he stared. Leaning her arms against the first step of the whirl-pool, she rested her head backward against the side of the concrete perimeter.

From his window, he saw her slick, shiny breasts encased in a black bathing-suit top. He wondered what she wore below, wishing she were completely naked. What he would give to take off that black little scrap of material and caress her with his hands and mouth. What he would give to slide bikini bottoms down her long, lithe legs and learn all her secrets.

Feeling the drumbeat of arousal in his blood, he stripped off his clothes and put on a swimsuit. His first instinct was to go nude, but he didn't want to frighten her away. Grabbing a towel, he headed downstairs and made his way to the hot tub.

He found her with her eyes closed and the steam rising around her, her hair slicked back, and he stepped into the tub. Her eyes flashed open and she sank deeper into the whirling bubbles.

"Rafe," she said. "I didn't know you were here."

"I just got here. You made it look irresistible."

"I probably should have simply gone to bed."

"Why?" he asked, his gaze dipping to her cleavage.

"I was tired."

"So you decided to take a relaxing dip in the Jacuzzi. That's why it's here."

She inhaled and let out a long sigh. "I guess you're right. I'm not used to treating myself."

"Maybe that's something you should change."

She shook her head. "Too much to do. When I get back to Atlanta, I'm sure I'll have a ton of work waiting for me."

"No need for you to rush back to Atlanta. You're doing something very important for Joel right here," he said. He wouldn't tell Nicole what he had planned for her and Joel yet. He knew he needed to break past several barriers before she agreed to his plan of staying at his place for Joel's security and for Rafe's pleasure.

"I know that," she said in a quiet, pensive voice.

"You've done a good job with him," he said.

"Thank you. He's a little shy and hesitant sometimes, but—"

"I noticed that. I think a karate class would be a good idea for him."

Nicole stared at him, splashing as she sat up. "Karate? He's too young for that. Besides, I'm very firm about teaching him to be nonviolent."

"Karate isn't violent," he said, surprised at her reaction. "It teaches discipline, physical fitness, self-control. All that fosters self-confidence." He remembered a time when he was young that his physical fitness had felt like the only thing he could control in his life. "You don't have him involved in any sports, do you?"

"No. I planned to enroll him in T-ball in the spring." She shook her head. "I can't agree to karate at this young age."

"He's A Medici," Rafe said. "At some point, he may run into people who, for whatever reason, resent me. I want him to be able to defend himself." He paused a half beat.

"Maybe it would help if you learned some self-defense techniques for yourself."

"Me?" she echoed, aghast. "Why would I want to do that?"

"So you could understand why I think this is a good idea for Joel." He shrugged. "I could teach you. I'm a black belt."

She met his gaze and a slice of fear cut through her eyes. "A black belt," she said, looking slightly ill. She shook her head. "I'm not really interested in learning karate. In fact, I'm really exhausted at the moment. I'm going up to bed."

She rose from the tub, the water dripping down the porcelain skin of her lean frame. She looked like a goddess rising from the water. He rose to his feet and noticed her swaying movement.

He immediately shot out his hands to steady her. "Are you okay?"

"I guess I got a little too relaxed." Her gaze dipped to his shoulders and chest then she blinked and looked away. In that second, he'd seen her covert admiration of his body. That Nicole, with all her reservations against him, was suffering a little lust in her heart gave him a rush. Touching the wet, naked skin of her waist made him hard.

"Let me help you out," he said, guiding her up the steps and grabbing her towel on the chair. He wrapped it around her and gave her arms a gentle squeeze. "There. Better get you inside or you'll get chilled. It's warm tonight, but not that warm."

While she stepped into a pair of flip-flops, he grabbed his own towel and gave himself a cursory rubdown. He ushered her inside the house and she stopped just inside the door.

"I'm okay now," she said in a low voice that made him wonder if she would sound that way in bed. "Thanks. And good night."

He watched her walk away, his gaze latching on to her bare legs and shoulders. Curling his fingers into a fist, he felt a punch of desire that surprised him. She was beautiful and classy, but so were other women. He liked the way she defended Joel like a mama bear. Her combination of toughness and sensual softness mesmerized him. He couldn't remember aching for a woman with such fierceness. Was it because she was turning him down?

The truth was Rafe didn't usually get turned down. Hell, for the most part, he didn't even have to ask. Women came to him, and they all knew he wasn't looking for anything serious or permanent. Although he'd confined his involvement to women who were both intelligent and beautiful, he could tell there was something different about Nicole. And he wanted a taste of it.

The next morning, Rafe's driver took Nicole and Joel to the preschool where they met a teacher and went for a tour. She was prepared to dislike it and searched for reasons to nix the choice, but the Montessori-based school was clean, the staff-to-student ratio optimal and most importantly, the children appeared happy and well-tended.

After their visit, Nicole and Joel returned home. While Joel rushed to the playroom, Nicole went to her bedroom and booted up her laptop, eager to check her email.

Sipping the perfect coffee brewed by Rafe's staff, she immediately noticed an email with an attachment from the P.I.

Her heart hammering in her chest, she downloaded the document and quickly read it. Rafe's history was laid out for her in black and white. His birth, his father's death and his subsequent displacement. His foster family had taken care of him as best they could, but they'd been unable to afford to send him to college. A football scholarship had helped him complete his education.

With unabashed curiosity, she read the rest of the report. He'd worked on yachts during summers off from high school and college. Before he acquired his first yacht, it appeared as if he'd worked nearly twenty hours per day. She couldn't help feeling impressed. Rafe had worked and lived the American dream.

Under his criminal records, he'd been charged with assault on five different occasions.

The notation stopped her cold.

Taking a deep breath, she tried to read the rest of the report, but she feared she might faint. Stepping away from her laptop, she sank on to the bed and tried to gather her wits.

Assault. Assault. Assault. Assault. Assault. She gulped at the thought. What had made Rafe use his fists? Did that mean he would use them again? On Joel?

A cold chill rushed through her.

She could not let Rafe hurt Joel. She would do anything to stop him.

Returning to her laptop, she read the rest of the report. She should operate from truth. Rafe had been a bouncer for two of the hottest clubs in Miami. His charges had all been related to his job and they'd all been dismissed. Perhaps that should have made her relax, but it didn't.

If Rafe was capable of violence, how would he use his strength against her or Joel? The instinct to take Joel and run roiled through her. If Rafe ever found out she was even thinking of running away with Joel, he would never let her near his son again. She was totally trapped unless she purchased flexible flights. Nicole printed off the investigator's report then conducted a search for a schedule of flights that left Miami for international destinations. She placed her passport with Joel's in the drawer and locked it. She needed all of this available for use at a moment's notice if Rafe threatened Joel.

The rest of the week, Rafe must have arrived home after Nicole went to sleep and left before she rose. Although Nicole didn't trust Rafe with Joel, she mentally gave him a black mark for not spending more time with Joel. If he was going to ignore his son, why should Joel move here?

The chauffeur drove Nicole and Joel to preschool and Nicole kissed him good-bye. The sight of him uncertainly entering his schoolroom tugged at her heartstrings. If only Rafe hadn't reappeared, Joel would be safe and secure in his own comfort zone in Atlanta.

She swam several laps in the pool in hopes of reducing her frustration. In other circumstances, she would welcome this time as a long-delayed break, but the situation was far too complicated for her to relax.

Her cell phone rang and she noticed the incoming call was from Rafe. She felt a spurt of adrenaline. "Hello," she said.

"Hi. How are you?"

"Fine, and you?" she asked, keeping her tone cool.

A brief silence followed. "You don't sound fine. What's wrong? Is the new assistant okay? What about Joel?"

"Everyone is fine. Joel is at school."

"Oh, bored?"

Standing, she paced around the pool. "No, but I am used to working."

"In that, you and I are the same. I've got a good distraction coming. I'm going to take you and Joel for a cruise on Friday evening. We won't return until Saturday night."

Surprise rushed through her. "Really? You're so busy. I wouldn't have thought you could make the time for this kind of trip?"

"I'm making the time. Just pack what the two of you will need. In the meantime, if you're really bored, you could do some shopping to furnish the house."

Nicole blinked. "Shopping. Why me?"

"I'm still making up from the time I spent in Atlanta. I hope to be caught up next week. It would be a huge favor to me if you would take care of it."

"But I don't know your taste," she protested.

"I trust you," he said, and she felt a stab of bitterness that she couldn't trust him in return.

"I don't know much about the shopping down here," she said.

"No problem. Just give Maddie a call and she can fill you in. See you tomorrow night."

Just before dusk, Rafe welcomed Joel and Nicole on to his yacht. He gave them the grand tour and enjoyed Joel's enthusiasm. Joel was especially excited to see the engine room and the game room. The three of them were served dinner and watched the lights as they left the harbor.

Joel was so wound up that it took him a while to settle down.

"I'll read the bedtime stories tonight," he said to Nicole.

She hesitated then nodded. "Okay."

Rafe had made the offer impulsively, but as soon as Joel sank down on the bed beside him with a book, he realized why he'd wanted the good-night time with his son. As he read the story about the big strawberry and the little mouse, he remembered piling into a bed with his brothers and listening to his father's deep voice as he told stories. His father had made them up on his own, stories of adventure that had evoked his imagination. He and his brothers had competed for the positions on his father's left and right side. Rafe couldn't remember a time when he'd felt more safe and secure.

Now, with his son curled against him, Rafe felt a wave of emotion at the bond forming between them. He wanted that sense of safety and security for Joel. He never wanted his son to experience the uncertainty he had.

"Do you like strawberries?" he asked Joel.

Joel gave a big nod. "I like them as much as the little mouse does. Again," he said. "Read it again."

Rafe laughed. "The same book?"

Joel nodded again. "It's the best book in the world," he said solemnly.

"Hmm," Rafe said, ruffling his fingers through Joel's hair. "Then I guess it's worth hearing again."

He started at the beginning and Joel moved his lips, wordlessly repeating each word of the story. The fact that his son had clearly memorized the book brought him enormous pride. Rafe ended up reading it yet another time, then he turned to another book. With Joel fully relaxed against him, Rafe glanced down and saw that his son was asleep.

His heart twisted. Joel's ability to let down his guard with him made something inside him swell with emotion. He wanted Joel to trust him. It was vital to him.

Gently, he tucked the covers over his son and slid out of bed, returning to the upper deck.

Nicole stood next to the side of the ship, looking into the distance.

He stepped beside her. "You think he liked his first day on the yacht?"

She turned to glance at him. "It was obvious he loved it."

"I'm glad he's a good sailor. I worried a little about seasickness and had both the meds and the sea bands ready for him just in case."

"That was thoughtful," she said.

"You sound surprised."

"You're a new dad. I wouldn't expect you to be prepared for everything."

"What about you? Do you like it out here?"

She inhaled. "Who wouldn't?"

"Someone who gets seasick."

She gave a low reluctant laugh that made him want to bend his head down and feel the sound against his skin. "It's so quiet and peaceful out here," she said.

"Right now it is. I've been out in some pretty rough storms where it's anything but peaceful."

"When did you first develop your fondness for boats or the ocean?"

"My father took us out a couple of times. I was very young, but I still remember it like it was yesterday." He thought of his father, his hair whipping in the wind as he called out instruction to him and his brothers. A wave of longing and nostalgia washed over him. "He was a good dad."

"In what way?" she asked and he felt her searching his face.

"Don't get me wrong. He could be tough as nails. With four sons and a wife who was—" He paused, feeling another twist of loss for his mother. "Fragile, he had to stay on top of everything. He taught us to work hard, taught us to swim and play poker. He even taught us all to cook."

She smiled. "Really?"

He nodded. "I can make some pretty mean spaghetti. He made great lasagna, but none of us can quite remember how to pull that together the same way he did."

She shook her head. "I'm not sure my mother or father know how to boil water."

"Different planet," he said.

"Not necessarily better," she muttered and looked out to the horizon. She gave a shiver.

He pulled off his jacket to put it around her shoulders. She glanced at him in surprise.

"You looked like you got a chill. I've been doing all the talking. How did a wealthy girl like you learn how to cook?"

"In boarding school. It was an elective and I decided it would be a necessary skill since I knew I wouldn't be living with my parents."

"Independent even then," he said.

"Yes," she said, her face solemn. "I think I was nine at the time."

"I get the impression your home life wasn't all that happy," he ventured.

"It wasn't. My parents were unhappily married. My father had a terrible temper. That may be part of the reason I'm so determined for Joel to feel safe and happy."

"You can't protect him from every bump in the road," Rafe said.

"No, but I can try to keep him out of the potholes," she said.

"Ever think you're overprotective?" he asked.

She shot him a look that reminded him of a mama bear ready to defend her cub. "Are you questioning my parenting skills?"

"Just curious," he said.

"Because if you are," she said. "You don't have a lot of experience yourself."

"I don't have experience being a parent," he agreed. "But I have experience being male."

"Plenty of single mothers have successfully raised boys on their own."

"But you won't have to," he said. "I'm Joel's father and I'm here to stay."

She lifted her shoulder. "We still don't know how involved you really want to be in his life."

Her cool response irritated him. "Very involved. You need to get used to the idea that Joel will be spending lots of time with me."

"Like I said, that's yet to be determined."

"No, it isn't," he said, putting his hand on her arm to get her attention.

She turned her head and glanced meaningfully at his hand. He removed it. "I'm not going to be an absentee father. I'm rearranging my life so that he can be in it all the time."

"It's not that easy," she said. "You can't just take over."

"I can and I am," he said.

"What do you mean?"

"I want Joel with me. You need to get used to the idea. I don't need your approval to get custody of my son."

Her eyes widened. "Are you threatening me?" She bit her lip. "Tabitha said you were a bully. This just goes to show—"

"Tabitha," he echoed in disgust. "The woman who laughed at me when I asked her to marry me."

Nicole gasped. "You proposed?" she asked in disbelief.

"She said I was good enough for a good time, but not for anything long-term. Then she didn't bother to tell me she was pregnant with my child. I could forgive her for that because she was so wild maybe she didn't know who the father was."

Nicole gasped again. "How dare you insult her when she's not here to defend herself?"

"She lost that right when she neglected to tell me she'd given birth to my son."

Nicole stared at him, her eyes glinting with fear and anger. "Why do you want him?" she demanded. "Is it your way of paying back my sister? Or is it some kind of ego trip?"

Offended by her assessment of his character, he ground his teeth. "I'll tell you when you have a more open mind. Now it's shut tighter than a jail cell."

"Don't underestimate me. I will do anything to protect Joel."

"Then you may want to be smart about it. You can waste your time fighting me, or you can officially move down here and work with me."

Her jaw dropped. "You've got to be kidding. Give up my life so you can control it and Joel's."

He gave a chuckle that sounded harsh to his own ears. "If you and I both really want what's best for Joel, why would I need to control you?"

She gnawed her lip for a moment then gave him his jacket. "Are you going to tell me that you're not accustomed to getting your way?"

"Only because I'm right most of the time," he said.

"That's arrogant."

"No, it's true." He ran his fingers through his hair in frustration. "When are you going to stop fighting me every inch of the way?"

"I agreed to come down here. I wasn't fighting then."

"I wouldn't take no for an answer."

"You don't make it easy. You march into our lives and want everything changed this second. It doesn't work that way. This is going to take time and trust."

"The time to start is *now*. Joel is young enough that if we move forward decisively then he'll feel secure in no time." Rafe knew what he was talking about. He'd been several years older than Joel when he'd lost his family, and he'd never fully recovered. "This can't be the worst offer you've received. Move to Miami and live in a nice house with a pool. You don't even have to work."

"I could have done that in Atlanta if I'd agreed to live with my father," she said with a trace of bitterness. "You're the same as he is. It all comes down to controlling other people to get your way."

"This isn't about control. This is about doing the right thing for Joel. You are the only mother Joel he has ever known. You're the one who has rocked him to sleep, kept him fed and warm. You're the one who has made him feel safe. Ideally, every child would have a caring father too. If you move down here, Joel would have the two most important people in his life together."

Six

Rafe made a good argument, Nicole thought after she'd returned to her room. She pulled the covers over her in her bed while the gentle rocking of the ocean lulled her. It would be best for Joel if she and Rafe could get along and even better if they lived together. But that was a fairy-tale possibility.

If only she could be sure that he was who he seemed to be. Strong, good-looking, gentle, responsible. He appeared to be every woman's dream come true. Even hers if she'd had the time to dream during the last four years.

But how could she possibly trust him? Especially after that report from the P.I. She would always feel like she needed to be on guard with him.

She wondered if he had truly been in love with her sister, or just infatuated. If he was who he seemed, how could Tabitha, even with her shallow nature, leave that kind of man behind? It didn't make sense to her. Although Tabitha had always talked about marrying a man both wealthy and famous, perhaps even royalty, Nicole had assumed it wasn't a serious plan.

After Tabitha had delivered Joel, she'd begun a strict exercise regimen to lose the baby weight, telling Nicole she had to get in shape for her prince. She'd partied frantically in New York, Los Angeles and Atlanta, refusing to slow down even when the doctor had insisted.

Nicole took a deep breath and sent up a silent wish of peace for her sister. Closing her eyes, she concentrated on the rhythmic rocking motion and allowed herself to drift to sleep.

Minutes later, he was in bed beside her. His wide shoulders blocked the bulk of the morning sun just beginning to rise. His rock-hard chest was inches from her. His dark, gold skin stretched over his well-developed muscles.

His physical strength fascinated her at the same time it frightened her. How could a man with such strength possess such gentleness?

His eyelids fluttered open and his dark gaze immediately latched on to her. "You're supposed to be sleeping," he said, sliding his hand under the covers to her bare hip. "I thought I took care of any nervous energy you had last night."

He lifted his index finger to her lips.

"I guess you haven't been kissed enough," he said and pulled her flush against his body.

Heat rushed through her and she couldn't stop a smile at the easy, sexy way he handled her. "I didn't say that. I was just looking at you."

"Why look when you can touch?" he asked and lifted one of her hands to his chest at the same time he lowered his mouth to hers.

His mouth sent fireworks through her. He seemed to devour her as if he couldn't get enough of her. He skimmed his mouth down over her shoulder, sending ripples of sensation in his wake.

He touched the sides of her breasts, teasing her until she couldn't remain still, pushing her nipples against his palm.

He swore under his breath, but it was a sound of pleasure. "I love the way you move."

Sliding one of his hands between her legs, he found her wet and swollen. "Ready already?"

A twinge of self-consciousness rushed through her. Did he really not know that he kept her in a state of readiness for him all the time? "Is that bad?" she asked, her voice sounding breathless to her own ears.

"If it's bad, then we're both bad," he said, and guided her hand over his erection.

She slid her hand over him, moving in long strokes.

He let out a hiss of breath, his eyes fixed on her. "I need you again."

It amazed her how powerful he could make her feel even when she was in such a vulnerable position. Suddenly, touching and needing weren't nearly enough. "I need you, too."

He rolled on to his back, pulling her on top of him, sending her equilibrium spinning. "You set the pace. If I do, it will all be over in sixty seconds."

She laughed despite her own mind-blowing arousal. Pushing herself up and propping her hands on either side of his head, she stared into his eyes as he wrapped his hands around her hips and guided her just over him.

"Take it slow," he told her. "You do wicked things to my self-control."

Sliding down him inch by delicious inch, she felt his groan vibrate inside her. She'd never imagined she could feel this free with a man, this desirable, this passionate, this...in love...

Nicole awakened so slowly she almost felt as if she were still dreaming. She heard the sound of laughter. *Joel,* she realized with a smile. She would know that sound anywhere. A second later, she heard a deeper, masculine chuckle. She blinked, immediately identifying Rafe's voice.

Disoriented, she sat up in bed, trying to make sense of the hot visual she'd had. Had Rafe been in her bed? Her body felt odd, swollen with arousal. She ran her hands over her night clothes and embarrassment washed over her.

What was the matter with her? How could she be having erotic dreams about a man she didn't trust? Or was it possible that her feelings for him were more complex than she'd realized? She shook her head, unable to believe it.

"Shhh. Don't wake your mother," Rafe said just outside her door.

"She likes me to wake her up," Joel said. "She likes it when I jump on the bed. It makes her laugh. You can come, too."

Still horrified by her dreams, Nicole gasped, scrambling out of bed and rushing to open the door. "I hear someone laughing," she managed, focusing on Joel, who was still dressed in his dinosaur jammies.

"It was me and him," he said, pointing at Rafe.

Dressed in shorts and a black T-shirt that stretched tight over his shoulders, Rafe stepped forward and leaned against the doorjamb in the hallway, stealing her attention and her breath.

"Somebody's a pistol in the morning," he said, giving her a swift, but thorough onceover before he met her gaze.

"He wakes up happy," she said, feeling self-conscious. "Don't you, Joel?"

He rushed into her arms and she hugged his sweet little body and gave him a good tickle. His belly laugh made her smile.

"If we could bottle that sound," Rafe said.

She nodded in agreement and hugged him again.

"Mom, we're gonna have pancakes. With strawberries and chocolate chips."

"Not in the same pancakes," Rafe corrected and rubbed his hand over Joel's head. "Tell her what else we're going to do."

"Fish," Joel said. "We're gonna catch fish."

His enthusiasm was contagious. "What are you going to do with them after you catch them?"

Joel looked at her then up at Rafe. "What do we do after we catch them?"

"We throw them back so someone else can take a turn catching them?"

Joel's face crinkled in confusion. "Can't I keep just one?"

"We'll see," Rafe said.

"That means no," Joel said in a glum tone.

"Maybe I could get an aquarium," Rafe ventured, lifting his thumb to his lip.

"An aquarium is a big commitment. Maybe we could just pick up one of those betta fish," Nicole said.

"That's okay. I'm in it for the long haul," Rafe said, and picked up Joel.

Nicole was struck by the resemblance between the two. With the exception of Joel's blue eyes, he could have been a miniature replica. It wasn't the first time she'd noticed their similarities, but every time seemed to underline their bond more and more. She took a quick breath and focused on his comment. "I'm speaking of someone else's interest. It wanes quickly."

"Ah," Rafe said. "Point taken. Betta fish on the way home. Are you joining us?"

"After I get dressed."

"No need," he said, his gaze skimming over her again. "We're casual."

"I'll be out soon," she said and closed her door. Her heart was racing. She frowned at herself, still disturbed by her hot dream. "Get a grip," she whispered.

Joel didn't stop bouncing with excitement for most of the day. His son even reached for his hand several times. The gesture tugged at his heart and he was relieved at the small sign of Joel's trust. Joel would adjust. His son would grow to trust him more each day, to rely on him, maybe even to love him. It would happen faster if he had Nicole's support and Rafe sensed he was getting to her.

She laughed and he felt her gaze on him several times throughout the day. He sensed both curiosity and skepticism. The latter made him impatient.

That night, after they returned to the house, Joel hit the sack early and Rafe took advantage of the time by inviting Nicole to join him for dinner on the patio.

"Have you ever gotten into a physical altercation as an adult?" Nicole asked him after dinner.

It was approximately the twentieth question she'd asked him regarding physical fights.

"Yes, I have. I was a bouncer for a couple of clubs in Miami. A few times I had to resort to brute strength, but not since. Why do you ask?" He met her gaze directly.

She bit her lip. "I just wanted to know what your approach to life was. If you thought physical intimidation was necessary."

"In rare circumstances. If someone came at you or Joel, I would defend you," he said. "I wouldn't be a man if I didn't."

"What do you mean—not a man?" she asked.

"I mean I wouldn't stand for anyone attacking you." He shrugged. "I would protect my son. My son's mother."

She stared at him for a long moment. "And what about your son? Would you physically punish him? Would you—" She broke off as if she could barely complete her sentence. "Would you punish a woman?"

Rafe scowled in distaste. "A real man never uses his strength against a child or a woman."

She bit her lip again. "You really believe that," she said in an unsteady voice.

"Of course I do. Only cowards prey on those who are weaker." He wondered where her questions originated. "Where is all of this coming from?"

She glanced away. "It was a philosophical question," she said.

"It sounded like more," he said.

She lifted her shoulders. "If you are going to be a partner in Joel's care, then I need to know what to expect. People have different philosophies about physical punishment."

He studied her for a long moment. "So you're afraid I'll beat him?"

Her heart skipped and her stomach knotted. She swallowed over the knot of emotion in the back of her throat. "I need to make sure I understand what you believe."

"We've talked about this before. I was spanked as a child, but I don't think it hurt me. I think there are better ways of disciplining children. My primary goal is protecting my child."

He spoke as if he were a modern-day warrior. Nicole tried to compute his words, but struggled to separate them from her father's actions.

"There's something you're not telling me," he said, his eyes narrowed.

She looked away. "Your appearance in Joel's life has been so sudden."

"That wasn't by my choice," he said.

"I know. But you're not the only one who feels protective of Joel." She pushed her hair behind one ear and appeared as if she were debating something. "I'm not sure of what your values are, what you've been taught."

Rafe felt a familiar twist in his gut. "What you mean is that I wasn't raised in civilized society and in the cocoon of extreme wealth. You're starting to sound like your sister. I'm a little too rough around the edges. I'm not quite good enough for prime time. Right?"

Nicole's lips parted in a soft gasp. "No. I didn't mean that at—"

He lifted his hand. "Save it. I've heard it before more than once. My family was poor, but my father loved us. My mother just wasn't strong enough to keep it all together after my dad and Leo died. So, yes, I was shuffled off to a foster family, who wanted me partly because I brought in extra income. Didn't catch up with my brothers until the last few years. Sometimes it feels like my first nine years were just a dream." He paused a half beat and shook his head. "I pretended I belonged, but I never did. I don't even have pictures of my family," he muttered, then looked at her. "Your parents probably commissioned oil paintings of you and Tabitha every year of your life."

"There were a lot of photos," she admitted.

"None of this matters. What matters is Joel is my son and I'm going to take care of him. Good night," he said and knew he had to get out. The walls of his house felt as if they were closing in around him. Or maybe it was his own bones and ribs squeezing his guts into a knot.

He grabbed the keys to his car and stopped suddenly. He couldn't just pick up and go anymore. He had to think of Joel. He turned to Nicole. "I need to go for a drive," he said. "I'll make sure the housekeeper keeps an ear out for Joel. I'll have my cell. Call me if you need me."

She nodded. "I think I gave you the wrong impression," she began.

"Not likely," he said, hearing the edge of cynicism in his own voice. "I'll be back in a few hours."

Sliding into his vintage Corvette, Rafe put the top down and headed for the pier. The wind blew over his face, assuaging just a tinge of his restlessness. Nicole's lack of trust in him drove him to a level of frustration he hadn't experienced in years, if ever.

He knew she wanted him, but she kept pulling back. She got under his skin even more than Tabitha had. He shook his head at the thought. No, he'd allowed himself to fall ass over teakettle for Tabitha. Rafe had more self-control these days. Lust was just another word for love.

It shouldn't bother him that she shared the same attitude about his lack of so-called class that Tabitha had, but it did.

A bitter taste filled his mouth. He could have dismissed any other woman, but this was Joel's mother.

Whether he liked it or not, he would have to bring her around to his way of thinking.

Nicole had never felt so conflicted in her life. Although she knew she was completely justified in making sure that Rafe would be a good parent to Joel, she hated the idea of causing Rafe pain. Given his history with her sister, her feelings were pure insanity.

Why did she care about hurting him? Was it because Rafe was Joel's father? Nicole suspected it was more than that. Something about Rafe made her feel longings she'd dismissed. She should forget those same longings now.

Five days later, a social-services specialist called the house to schedule a visit. Nicole reluctantly called Rafe.

"What does she want?" he asked.

"She wants to observe Joel and you to see how he is adjusting," Nicole said, pacing as she talked to him. The two of them had barely exchanged a word since he'd taken off that night after her confrontation.

"What did you tell her?" he demanded.

"I told her that you and Joel had a wonderful time on your yacht," she said. "But you haven't given me any new material since then."

"You told her that?" he said, fury in his voice.

Nicole shook her head in exasperation. "Just the first part. But it would have been the truth. You don't seem to grasp the concept that fathering is an everyday commitment, not just an every-now-and-then exercise."

"I'm still catching up from my time in Atlanta," he said in a clipped voice, then swore. "When is she coming?"

"I wanted to ask you first so you could be prepared," she said.

Silence hung between them. "Thank you," he said. "How about Saturday?"

"I don't think they like to work weekends," she said.

"Okay," he said and paused. "Tuesday," he said. "Tuesday afternoon. We'll spend some time in the pool. Joel likes that. We'll go out on the yacht again on Friday."

Nicole packed for Joel and herself and met Rafe again at the dock. Something raw and unspoken passed between them. Rafe extended his hand to Joel and her son hesitantly took it.

Rafe shot her a look of inquiry.

"A day is a week to a three-year-old," she said.

"Good point."

Rafe worked at charming his son and by evening, Joel allowed him to read his bedtime stories. Nicole paced the deck, full of conflicting emotions. She wished the wind whipping through her would bring clarity with it.

"What have you told him about me?" Rafe asked from behind her.

She closed her eyes and crossed her arms over her chest. "That you're busy working. You have a very important job and a lot of people depend on you."

"It doesn't wash, does it?" he said more than asked, moving beside her.

"It will for a little bit, then not so much," she said and met his gaze. "Fatherhood is a huge time commitment. I'm not sure you're ready for it."

He narrowed his eyes. "Is that what you told the social-services specialist?"

"Absolutely not," she said.

"Why not, if it's what you believe?"

She looked away and shrugged. "You're new at this, so you're bound to screw up."

Silence followed. "Excuse me?"

She met his gaze. "Think about it. How much training have you had to be a father?"

"None, but—"

"Exactly, and like most people, you probably think it should come naturally. But it doesn't. It takes work."

The wind whipped through his hair. "If I were in your position, I might be tempted to sabotage me."

"It has occurred to me," she said without blinking.

His eyes widened. "Then why haven't you?"

She sighed. "Several reasons. It ultimately wouldn't be best for Joel. And you seem to be sabotaging yourself. You don't need my help."

His mouth lifted in a half grimace. "This is where you are nothing like your sister."

"Is that a compliment or insult?" she asked. "I'm not always sure."

"Compliment," he said. "Your honesty is one of your most seductive qualities."

Nicole held her breath, unable to summon a pithy retort. Damn it if she hadn't missed him, too. It made no sense.

"We need to work together on this," he said, taking her hand and lifting it to his lips.

Her heart jumped. "Working together implies two people, not just one."

He lifted a dark eyebrow. "Are you saying I'm a slacker?"

She bit her lip to keep from smiling at his charm. "I haven't been MIA for five days."

"You noticed," he said. "And you counted the days."

"For Joel's sake," she said.

He gave a slow nod. "Point taken."

The next day Rafe and Joel fished. Rafe even cajoled Nicole into trying her hand at it. He couldn't help laughing at her squeal of victory when she caught a fish.

As they headed to the dock, he spotted Maddie waiting. "Damn," he muttered. "Haven't been gone twenty-four hours."

"What's wrong?" Nicole asked, coming from behind him.

"Maddie," he said. "That usually means there's something that needs my attention. Immediately," he added, surprised at his disappointment. He'd been planning a quiet evening with Joel and Nicole.

"She doesn't really look dressed for work," Nicole said.

Rafe noticed his assistant's black dress and shrugged. "Maybe she has a party."

Maddie waved as the pilot parked the boat. A member of the staff lowered the gang plank steps and she immediately boarded the yacht. "Welcome back. I thought I should wait until you returned to tell you that the Crawford deal is in jeopardy. He's in Fort Lauderdale this weekend for that charity event you helped sponsor, so you'll be able to take a quick trip up there and smooth the waters. I can drive you if you like."

He shook his head, mentally planning how to shorten the trip. "Nah, that's okay. I'll either drive myself or get Dan to take me. Is that the event for veterans?"

"Yes, it is," she said, appearing disappointed. "Are you sure you don't want me to drive you? It's no problem."

"No," he said. "Veterans," he repeated and glanced at Nicole. "Any chance you want to go?"

Nicole blinked in surprise. "What kind of event is it?"

"It's an event put on by a yacht club in Fort Lauderdale to

raise money for veterans suffering from post-traumatic stress syndrome. You know who's speaking?" he asked Maddie.

She paused, then sighed. "Gerard something," she said.

"Gerard Thomas," Nicole said, smiling. "I've worked with him before. He's a terrific speaker."

"Then join me," he said, meeting her gaze.

Nicole glanced in Maddie's direction then back at him. "Are you sure?"

"Yeah."

"What about Joel?" Maddie asked. "I mean, do you think he'll be uncomfortable being left at home without Nicole?"

"I think that one's headed for an early bedtime, and this occasion is one of the reasons we have a mother's helper." He brushed his hands together. "Decision made. Nicole's coming with me."

"I think Maddie was disappointed that you chose not to take her tonight," Nicole said as Dan, Rafe's chauffeur, drove Rafe's limo toward Fort Lauderdale. She and Rafe had quickly changed clothes at Rafe's house before they left.

"Why?" he asked, unbuttoning his jacket. "It meant she had a night off. Besides, this gives me yet another opportunity to show off the advantages of southern Florida."

Nicole wondered again about Rafe's relationship with his assistant, but didn't want to pry. "If you're trying to sell me on it," she began.

"Yeah?" he prompted.

"Today was very nice," she said.

"Very nice," he gently mocked. "The temperature in Atlanta was thirty-nine with drizzle."

"Okay, you've got Atlanta beat in the weather department—except during hurricane season."

"If a hurricane hits, we can visit my brother in Atlanta or my other brother in Las Vegas. Or Aspen. I have a place there. If you really want to get out of Dodge, we can go to Italy. Damien worked out some kind of arrangement for a chateau where my ancestors lived."

"That sounds interesting," she said, remembering the life of luxury she'd led when she'd lived with her father. "How long ago did your family live there?"

"About two hundred and fifty years before my grandfather made a bad business arrangement and was swindled out of the family home."

"That's terrible."

"Yes, it was, but it forced my father to come to America, which meant I was born here. I'm glad for that. Your ancestry goes back pretty far, too, doesn't it? Bet you're a member of a few exclusive ladies' societies," he said.

Nicole had never focused much on her so-called pedigree. There were too many more important things. "I guess, but my membership has probably lapsed. Oh, darn," she said in a mocking voice.

He smiled at her. "I would have sworn you never missed a meeting."

"Then you would have been wrong. Not that there's anything wrong with the organization. They do some wonderful things, grant scholarships, perform charitable work…"

"How many meetings did you attend?"

"A few during breaks from college. My mother and father made it compulsory."

"When did you stop going?"

"The second after I moved out on my own for good."

"You did that in one year," he remembered.

"You're quoting the résumé you got from your P.I.," she

said, feeling a twinge of guilt that she hadn't told Rafe about the report she'd received about him.

"Yeah," he said. "You pretty much flipped the bird at your parents as soon as you got out. How did you manage to buy your house so quickly?"

"I'm surprised you didn't get that information, too," she said. "My grandfather on my mother's side left me a small trust. I quickly learned the joys of economizing."

"You and I have more in common than you think. I learned the *so-called joys of economizing* early. You learned them later. I bet that wasn't easy."

"I actually had to read a few books on the subject," she confessed. "Need versus want. I learned to budget." She laughed. "Tabitha considered the word budget profane."

"I can see that. I went shopping with her in South Beach a few times."

"You went shopping with my sister?" Nicole said in surprise. It was hard for her to imagine Rafe indulging her sister to such a degree.

"Jewelry shopping," he said. "She wanted diamonds, but never in the form of a ring."

"Oh," Nicole said, and actually felt embarrassed for her sister's greedy behavior. "Sorry."

"You live and learn. At one time, I would have said it was part of her charm."

"And now?"

"Tabitha was a taker."

Nicole couldn't defend her sister, because what Rafe said was partly true.

"Very different from you," he said, studying her. "I wonder what would have happened if I'd met you first."

"It wouldn't have made any difference," Nicole said,

sitting back, after she realized she'd been leaning toward him, her hand inches from his knee. "We've already discussed this. Tabitha was like a flower to bees when it came to attracting men."

"The challenge with Tabitha was to keep her entertained," he said. "With you, the challenge is getting in the door. I can see through the window," he said, sliding his hand over her brow. "There's a lot inside."

"Not worth the trouble," she said lightly, despite the fact that she felt herself tremble.

He shook his head and rubbed his thumb over her lip. "You're a terrible liar, Nicole. I like that about you."

After Rafe and Nicole arrived at the charity function, Rafe introduced Nicole to his business acquaintances and she excused herself to say hello to the speaker. He couldn't help but notice her enthusiasm as she talked with the man, and fought an odd jab of irritation.

Rafe turned back to his client and was displeased to learn that he'd been having talks with Nicole's father. He wondered if Nicole had somehow picked up on one of his conversations and leaked some information to her father. Would she help her father steal one of his deals? The possibility made his blood boil.

As Nicole walked toward him, he decided to conduct a test. "Nicole, I'd like you to meet Derek Crawford. Derek owns a yacht-leasing company and we've been working together for the last month."

Derek, a middle-aged man with a huge ego, appeared to stand a little straighter at the sight of Nicole.

"Derek, this is Nicole Livingstone," Rafe said and watched both Nicole and Crawford. Crawford's smile dipped slightly.

"Livingstone," he repeated and cleared his throat. "What a coincidence. You wouldn't be related to Conrad Livingstone Yachts, would you?"

Nicole nodded. "He's my father," she said and accepted the man's hand. "It's nice to meet you. Rafe tells me you're an astute businessman, so I can see why you enjoy working with him."

"And what would you say of your father?" Crawford asked with a cagey smile.

"My father kept his business separate from family, so I don't have any real experience. He's obviously been successful, though," she said in a neutral tone. "Do you live in Fort Lauderdale most of the year?"

"Since I own several yachts, I live anywhere I want. How did you meet Medici if not through your father?"

Nicole hesitated. "Through my late sister, actually. Oh," she said glancing toward the crowd of people moving toward the seats. "It looks like they're getting ready to start the keynote. Pleasure to meet you, Mr. Crawford."

"All mine," he said then looked at Rafe and lifted his eyebrows. "I'll be in touch. Can't beat the combination of a Livingstone and a Medici."

"Ladies and gentlemen, please take your seats in preparation for our guest speaker," a man at the front of the room announced.

"That's our cue," he said and led Nicole to their table at the front.

She stiffened at his touch. "Is that the reason you wanted me to come tonight? Because you're competing on this deal with my father?"

"What are you talking about?" he asked in a low voice.

"Is the reason you wanted me to join you tonight so you

could parade Conrad Livingstone's daughter in front of the competition? Your chance to use me to get ahead?"

He narrowed his eyes. "On the contrary. The first I heard about your father trying to steal my deal was through Crawford tonight. I wondered if you had overheard me and warned your father so he could make a deal."

Her jaw dropped in gratifying shock and Rafe had his answer. Nicole hadn't tried to sabotage his business deal.

Anger glinted through her blue eyes. "You don't know me at all," she said and turned her attention to the speaker.

Throughout the speech, he could feel her seething in her seat. While he was tempted to escort her out of the room so they could settle this once and for all, Rafe bided his time. They had the entire drive back to South Beach.

The second the speech ended, Nicole sprang from her chair. Rafe joined her, circling her wrist lightly with his fingers.

She turned her head to glance meaningfully at his hand. "I want to say hello to the speaker."

"Introduce me," he challenged.

She exhaled in frustration and tugged her hand away from his, going to the front of the room. "Great job, Gerard, as usual."

The rough-hewn man with shaven head cracked a grin. He stepped toward Nicole, and Rafe noticed a slight limp. "Always glad to get praise from Atlanta's prettiest peach. I only got to talk to you for a minute before my speech. I didn't get to ask you what you're doing down here."

Gerard glanced past her shoulder, meeting Rafe's gaze. "Are you with—"

"Nicole is with me," Rafe said, extending his hand. "Rafe Medici."

Nicole tossed him a sideways glance. "This is Gerard Thomas. I would say he's ex-marine, but—"

"Once a marine, always a marine," Rafe finished for her.

Gerard nodded, his gaze observant as he appeared to assess the relationship between Nicole and Rafe. "Is this a permanent move?"

"Not—" Nicole began.

"I'm working on it," Rafe said.

"It's complicated. Rafe is Joel's biological father."

"Oh. I didn't know he was in the picture."

"I am now," Rafe said.

"It's a transition period. Rafe lives in South Beach."

Gerard nodded. "I'd hate to see the veterans in Atlanta lose you."

"Nothing is settled," she said.

"I don't live far from here, so give me a call if you decide you want to work down here." He turned to Rafe. "Nice meeting you, Mr. Medici. We all think a lot of Nicole. She's a special woman. Joel has always been her number-one priority."

"He still is. Good meeting you," Rafe said, stepping aside with Nicole as other people pushed forward to speak with Gerard. "Ready to go?" he asked Nicole.

She gave a single mute nod and he sent a programmed text to the chauffeur. As they walked outside, the limo appeared and Dan quickly opened the door.

Rafe followed Nicole inside and set down the privacy panel. His cell rang and it was Maddie asking about the Crawford deal. "I have it under control," he said.

"Do you need me to come over in the morning for a briefing?" she asked. "I know this is a big deal."

"That won't be necessary. I'm staying on this one personally."

"Okay, I've found some more yachts on Grand Cayman you might be interested in. Would you like us to take a quick flight down tomorrow? I can make the arrangements."

Rafe glanced at Nicole, who had opened a bottle of water and was flipping through a magazine. "No. I have other plans."

"Okay, but I know how you hate to miss out on a good deal. I think some of these are distress sales."

"They can wait. I'll see you Monday morning," he said and turned off the phone. He allowed his gaze to rest on Nicole. Her sophisticated black dress dipped just low enough to draw his attention to her breasts. The sight of her silky brown hair made him want to feel it all over his naked skin. The possessiveness that tugged at his gut took him by surprise.

"Anything I should know about you and Gerard Thomas?"

She glanced up at him in surprise. "What do you mean? I've known him for about two years. He was seriously injured after 9/11 and was honorably discharged. He's a tireless advocate for veterans, and he's always been supportive of me and kind to Joel."

"Joel?" Rafe echoed. "When did he meet Joel?"

"A few times when he was in town. He always brought a toy."

"I thought you said you hadn't been involved with any men," he said.

"I haven't. Gerard's a colleague and friend."

"Who wanted and still wants more," Rafe said.

Nicole shrugged. "He may have asked me out a few times, but I didn't—" She broke off. "It wasn't good timing."

"Now?"

"Now, it's worse," she said, then frowned. "Why are you asking me this?"

"I think I should know if the mother of my child is involved with another man," he said.

"Well, I'm not," she said, laughing. "Not that it's really any of your business. You'll notice I haven't been asking you about women in your life."

"I've already told you I haven't had any serious involvements."

She gave a laugh. "Would that kind of response from me satisfy you? I haven't been involved seriously. Just a few sexual flings."

Rafe felt his gut take another twist. "Is that the truth?"

She groaned and looked upward. "I was kidding. I don't think it's fair for you to grill me when you have your own questionable relationships."

"Such as?" he asked.

She paused for a moment. "What about Maddie?"

"Maddie?" he echoed. "She's my assistant."

"Wasn't that her on the phone?" she asked and glanced at her watch. "Ten o'clock on a Saturday night?" She broke off and an odd expression crossed her face.

"What?" he asked.

"Nothing," she said, sipping her water. "I'm sure it was just a misunderstanding."

He gave a rough chuckle. "You're lying again. Go ahead and tell me what's going on in that brain of yours."

She hesitated, then shook her head. "It's none of my business."

"Nicole," he said, unable to keep impatience from his tone.

"Do the two of you have a history?" she asked.

He shrugged. "She's been working for me for years."

"I mean a romantic history," she said in a low voice.

Rafe blinked. "Hell, no. Why would I ruin a great business relationship just for sex?"

Nicole lifted her shoulders uncertainly. "Maybe she doesn't feel the same way. Have you considered that she may wish things were different?"

He rubbed his chin. "Never crossed my mind. I don't know why it would cross hers."

Nicole made a little sound of exasperation. "Maybe because you're extremely good-looking and wealthy. I think she has a crush on you."

Rafe considered the possibility for a moment and felt a barrage of misgivings. "God, I hope you're wrong. That would make things sticky as hell."

He considered the suggestion that Maddie might want a romantic relationship, then dismissed it. If Maddie had wanted him that way, she would have made her move long before now, and he was thankful she hadn't because he couldn't return the interest.

"Maddie is my assistant, nothing more. But my relationship with you is more complicated. You're the mother of my son. You need to trust me."

Seven

Nicole's heart hammered against her ribcage at the intensity in his expression. "It's too soon." She took a quick breath. "We need more time."

"Speak for yourself," he said.

She bit her lip. "I need more time."

He shrugged and stretched his neck as if he had a kink in it. Her hands itched to touch him. Maybe more. His muscles were seductive. His strength, nearly irresistible.

Clenching her hands to keep from touching him, she wondered why she was so drawn to him. She'd always been afraid of powerful men.

They rode the rest of the way home in silence. As each mile passed, Nicole became increasingly drowsy. She fought sleep, but it finally overtook her. Awakening as the limo pulled to a stop, she found herself slumped against Rafe, her head on his shoulder.

She lifted her head. "Sorry. I guess I was sleepier than I thought I was."

"No problem," he said, his voice a rumbling sexy tone. "You're not heavy."

She met his dark gaze and felt an odd weakness invade her. "Thank you for the time on the yacht. It was—" She inhaled as her throat closed up with some sort of strange anticipation or emotion. "Nice," she said.

"Yeah," he said and lowered his head as he splayed his fingers behind the nape of her neck. "Very nice." He pressed his mouth against hers and kissed her.

She should pull away, but he felt so good, so firm, so strong. Clinging to his shoulders, she held on as he took her mouth on a sensual journey of pleasure.

When he finally pulled away, she was gasping for air. "Um," she whispered.

He pressed his index finger against her lips. "Don't say anything. I don't understand what's happening between you and me. I just know something is. We'll figure it out. Okay?"

Unable to produce a sound, she nodded slowly. He had such a strange, potent effect on her. She knew she needed to remain in control. She needed to remain rational, but Rafe affected her on a cellular level, far beyond reason.

"Okay," she murmured and he helped her out of the car and up the stairs.

She turned to face him, feeling the solid door behind her. She needed the sensation of hard wood when her brain and heart felt like mush. "Thank you," she said.

"You are very welcome, Nicole," he said and cupped her jaw with a hand, massaging her mouth open. He slid his tongue inside, tasting her, taking her as much as he could, but letting her know that he wanted more, so much more.

Pulling back, he stared into her eyes. "Say the word and I'll stay with you tonight."

Her heart leapt into her throat and she couldn't have formed a sound if her life depended on it. Not even a word. Her breath locked somewhere between her throat and her lungs.

He slid his finger down her throat. "Another time, then," he said. "Another time and we'll be together in every possible way."

He walked away and she leaned against the door, praying her knees would hold her. Catching her breath, she mustered her strength. She pushed open her bedroom door and stumbled to the connecting bathroom. Turning on the light, she looked into the mirror and saw a woman with lips swollen from kisses, eyes nearly black with arousal and cheeks pink from heat. That woman was her. Nicole couldn't remember ever feeling this way.

She felt dizzy with want and need. Covering her hot cheeks with her hands, she tried to regain her equilibrium. She needed to rein in her wants and needs. More than ever, she needed to focus on what was right for Joel, but Rafe was turning into a constant craving.

The following day, she had little chance to pull her guard in place. Rafe played with Joel in the heated pool, and Joel begged her to join them. Rafe's gentleness with Joel chipped away at her defenses. Rafe taught Joel how to float, kick and dog paddle. After they ate sandwiches by the pool, Joel was tired enough for a nap.

Nicole took advantage of the downtime to rest in a chaise lounge beneath one of the large umbrellas. Feeling the weight shift in her chair, she opened her eyes to see

Rafe leaning over her. His hair still damp from the pool, his tanned, broad shoulders dotted with water, he brushed a strand of hair from her cheek.

"Looks like Mom is almost as tired as the kid," he said.

She nodded, closing her eyes to his effect on her, but she wasn't sure it worked. "Between the time on the yacht and the trip to Fort Lauderdale, I'm pooped."

"You like the sun, don't you?"

She nodded again. "The heat feels good. The breeze is delicious."

"Yeah," he said. "Did you know the temperature in Atlanta is forty-six?"

She met his taunting gaze. "You had to tell me that, didn't you?"

He gave a low chuckle that rippled through her. "I could make you like it here. A lot."

She closed her eyes. "I was relaxing until you started talking about Atlanta."

"If Atlanta makes you tense, then all the more reason to stay here," he said and covered her lips with his fingers before she could protest that *he* was making her tense. "Relax," he said. "You're here in the promised land."

She closed her eyes and tried not to think about what promises he could fulfill. She took a few deep breaths and drifted to sleep. Some time later, Joel appeared at her side and tugged at her arm.

"Wake up," Joel said. "We're gonna play Wii."

Blinking, Nicole sat up, noticing that a soft towel had been draped over her. Surprised at how quickly the time had passed, she pulled Joel close for a hug. "When did you wake up?"

"A long time ago. You've been sleeping forever. I asked

Daddy Rafe to wake you up, but he said to let you sleep. He put the blanket on you." He tapped his foot impatiently. "I want to play Wii."

Her heart stuttered at his reference to Rafe as Daddy. "Okay," she said, smiling at him. "Go play Wii and I'll get dressed."

"Are you okay?" he asked.

She glimpsed a slice of fear in his eyes. "Of course I am. I was just extra sleepy."

"You're not sick, are you?"

Nicole's heart twisted and she shook her head, taking him into her arms again. "No, sweetie. I just stayed up too late last night."

He let out a big sigh of relief. "Okay."

Nicole realized that more than ever she represented safety and security to Joel. What if something happened to her? What would happen to Joel? The possibility clawed at her. Even though she'd made backup plans, Nicole hated the idea of him feeling afraid and abandoned.

Her stomach pulled into a square knot. Even though she was still uncertain about Rafe, she could tell that he was determined to be responsible about his role as Joel's father. She would need to teach him.

Later that evening, after Joel went to bed, Nicole broached the subject with Rafe. "I need to tell you how to be Joel's father."

He shot her an incredulous look. "You're going to tell me how to be a father?"

"I'm going to educate you about your son's needs and how you can best take care of those needs," she said.

He crossed his arms over his chest. "I have some idea about what a boy needs."

"Your ideas may not be correct," she said. "For example, did you know that Joel reaches for his purple elephant whenever he's feeling insecure?"

Rafe's face fell. "Purple elephant?"

"His name is Fred," she said.

"Fred?"

She shrugged. "Joel likes orange juice and apple juice. When he eats too many sweets, he gets cranky. When he doesn't get to bed in time, he gets cranky."

"How many sweets?" Rafe asked. "What time to bed? Ten?"

"More than two cookies," she said. "Nine o'clock bedtime is pushing it. Eight o'clock is best. And as you saw yesterday, if he has a super-active day, he needs a nap. He does best with a schedule. You have to stick to it."

"Why are you telling me all of this?"

She suddenly felt a pain in her chest and struggled to take a breath. "Because you need to know these things if you're serious about being Joel's father. I may not always be around."

"Why not? Is this because you might want to take off with Gerard Thomas?"

"No," she said frustrated. "That's the last thing on my mind. You and I don't know how this situation is going to work out. And it hit me this afternoon that there are no guarantees. If something were to happen to me, Joel wouldn't go to my cousin, Julia. He would be with you, and I can't bear the thought of him feeling insecure or abandoned."

He moved toward her and took her in his arms. "Nothing is going to happen to you. You're going to be fine. You're going to nag Joel for the rest of his life."

Feeling his strong arms around her, she couldn't stop tears from filling her eyes. She bit her lip and tried to laugh to cover her emotion. "I like to think so, but you and I both know that there are no guarantees. You still need to learn what Joel needs."

"I know. I know," he said. "But right now, this woman needs to go to bed."

Allowing him to lead her up the stairs to her room, she was surprised at how much she craved his tenderness. It took her by surprise. Perhaps because her father had given her so little compassion.

Rafe escorted her into the room and urged her down on to the bed. She sat, looking up at him. "I need to brush my teeth."

"You want me to undress you?" he asked with a wolfish expression.

She smiled and shook her head. "You need to give me a break. I can't take you on now."

"Damn. If I had a little less integrity, I would have my wicked way with you."

"If I stayed awake," she said.

"Oh, you would stay awake," he said with a dark need in his gaze that made her feel as if she'd touched a live electrical wire. "I promise."

Her stomach dipped at the way he looked at her. She pushed herself to send him away. "Thanks for helping me upstairs. G'night."

He brushed a strand of her hair from her forehead and she couldn't withhold a sigh. "G'night. Call me if you need me."

She shook her head, unable to keep a slight smile from her face. "G'night," she said with more finality than she would have thought possible.

* * *

Rafe couldn't sleep. His mind weighed heavy with the responsibility of Joel and Nicole. In theory, she wasn't his responsibility, but in his reality, she was.

Keeping the door to his suite open, he paced his room keeping an ear out for Joel just in case his son awakened in the middle of the night. *His son.* Sometimes he still couldn't believe it. He was caught between an indescribable joy and terror, but Rafe was determined to be the father he'd lost. Nothing would keep him from it.

He went to the bar in his room and poured himself a shot of Scotch. He tossed back the liquor and felt it burn all the way down his throat. The thought of Nicole burned him in a different way.

For convenience's sake, he wanted to take her. It would be easier if she was on his side concerning Joel. But that wasn't all. She made him hot and bothered. He downed another shot and paced his suite.

He heard a sound, a loud moan, and stopped his pacing. A few seconds later, he heard, "No! No!"

Recognizing Nicole's voice, he headed for her bedroom. She gave a loud shriek. Another. His gut twisted at the sound of fear and desperation and he entered her bedroom.

She tossed and turned, screaming. He immediately climbed into bed and took her into his arms.

"Help," she called in a voice that stabbed at his heart, her arms splaying around him.

"I'm here," he said, holding her against him. "I've got you. You're safe."

"I can't breathe. I can't—" she said, clearly disoriented as she clung to him.

"You're okay. I'll keep you safe." He held her tight.

She took several deep breaths then opened her eyes and met his gaze. "Rafe?"

"Yes. You had a nightmare."

"I dreamed I was in the hospital. I couldn't breathe. Joel was crying." She let out a ragged breath. "I'm sorry."

"Don't apologize." He felt her strain to get close to him and something inside him seemed to shift.

Moments passed before her breath turned to normal. "I should tell you to go," she whispered.

His heart hammered against his chest.

"But I can't."

Later, surrounded by darkness, Nicole awakened to the sensation of Rafe's arms still wrapped protectively around her. Disconcerted, she tried to recall why he was in her bed, but reality smudged together with frightening dreams.

Rafe's hard chest meshed with her breasts. Her legs twined through his.

She supposed she could have pulled away from him, but she wasn't at all inclined. Instead, she buried her face in his throat and lifted her hands to his shoulders. She'd always been afraid of his kind of strength before, but at this moment, she wasn't. At this moment, she craved it.

Groaning, he lowered his hands to her hips.

Nicole sucked in a sharp breath and went still.

He squeezed her hips and drew her into his crotch.

Oh.

Help.

"You feel so good," he muttered, rubbing his mouth over her hair.

Her pulse skittered inside her. More than anything, she wanted him closer. He could protect her, make her feel safe.

He thrust against her and she felt his hardness. "I want you," he muttered against her throat.

She wondered if he was fully awake, but part of her didn't care. He felt so powerful, strong and good.

He touched one of her breasts and hesitated. He swore. "I want to be inside you," he said. "As deep as I can get." His body shuddered against hers. "Are you sure you want this?" he asked, slipping his hand beneath her chin and lifting it so she would meet his dark, sensuous gaze. "Are you sure you want me to take you?"

She trembled inside and out. No hiding now, she thought, his sense of honor doing crazy things to her. "Yes, I do," she whispered. "I do."

He pulled down her panties and his boxers and seconds later, she felt him rubbing against her where she was wet and swollen. He cupped her breasts and stroked her nipples. The friction of him against her most sensitive place stole her breath.

Arching against him, she spread her thighs, aching for him.

He stroked her with his fingers and took her mouth in an endless kiss that made her feel as if she were drowning. With each caress from his hands and mouth, she grew more restless.

"Rafe," she said, the husky sound matching her need.

He knew what she needed and thrust inside her with one delicious, filling stroke.

"Oh," she moaned.

"Oh," he echoed and swore. With a mind-robbing rhythm, he sent her over the top and followed after.

Eight

Nicole closed her eyes as she tried to catch her breath. Lying beside Rafe, she couldn't believe how fast—how easily... She gulped in another breath of air, desperately seeking some measure of sanity.

Their coupling had been so primitive and passionate. Taking him and being taken by him had blown the after-effects of her nightmare clear to smithereens. How could she have gone from complete terror to pleasure to some sort of strange peace in minutes? How could he affect her so powerfully?

A stab of vulnerability shot through her.

As if he knew, his hand wrapped around hers. After their house-on-fire lovemaking, the tenderness of his gesture made her feel like weeping. She took a deep breath to keep the tears at bay.

"You okay?" he asked in a low voice.

She nodded, but the gravity of the step she'd just taken began to sink in. "We didn't use protection," she whispered, pulling her hand away from his and sitting up.

"Yeah, I know," he said, sitting up, too.

Panic raced through her. "Oh, my God."

He put his hands on her shoulders. "Hey, there's no need to go crazy. One time without contraception doesn't guarantee a pregnancy."

His words offered little comfort. "No, but—"

"If it does happen, we can get married," he said calmly.

She gaped at him in shock. "Married," she echoed and began to shake her head.

"It's not the worst thing in the world. You and I have something big in common. Joel. That's more than a lot of people getting married have in common."

"But we hardly even know each other. We don't love each other."

He dropped his hands from her shoulders and shrugged. "So, what's love anyway? Intense lust? I think we proved we have that for each other."

Appalled by his cavalier attitude, she shook her head. "You don't believe in love?"

A shadow of cynicism crossed his face. "I thought I did one time. I was wrong."

He was speaking of Tabitha. He'd thought he was in love with her. Her stomach gave a vicious wrench. For an awful second, she feared she was some kind of substitution for her sister. Suddenly feeling overexposed in every way, she pulled the bedspread over her.

"Cold?" he asked.

She nodded, but the feeling wasn't just physical. "I—

uh." She cleared her throat. "This is awkward, but I need to be alone."

"Buyer's remorse?" he asked, still beautifully, unabashedly naked.

She bit her lip. "Overwhelmed. It happened so fast. I didn't think it through."

"Are you suggesting that I pushed you? Because—"

"No," she said. "If anything it was the opposite. That dream was so frightening. I was desperate to feel alive."

"Any man would do?" he asked, lifting a dark brow.

"Of course not." She sighed. "I'm not myself. I'm rattled. I need—" She took another breath. "I need some time alone."

"Okay," he said, touching his finger to her nose. "But be forewarned, if you start screaming again, I'm coming in here."

She smiled, but suspected it came across as more of a grimace. "No more screaming."

He shot her a look full of sensual promise as he rose from the bed. "No need to be rash. Under the right circumstances, screaming can be good."

She forced herself to look away from him as he pulled on his boxers. He caught her by surprise when he slid his hand beneath her chin and kissed her. "Don't worry. Things could be much worse," he said, then left her to sort out her thoughts.

After he left, she waited for herself to settle down, to become rational again. Even though she'd known she was attracted to Rafe, there were so many reasons for her not to give in to her feelings.

First, she needed to remain objective for Joel's sake. She still needed to find out if Rafe had any potential of being abusive, and if she did, she would fight to the death to keep him away from Joel. Secondly, her sister had been involved with Rafe. She'd always stayed away from men who'd dated Tabitha. If a man fell for Tabitha, then he couldn't possibly be right for Nicole. She was too different. Beyond those two mountains of objections, she'd just learned that Rafe didn't believe in love. Did she want to spend her entire life with such a cynical man?

Nicole's head began to ache. Torn in a dozen different directions, she climbed out of bed and took a shower in the adjoining bathroom. Maybe the water could wash away her confusion.

The following morning, Nicole had to drag herself out of bed. After urging Joel to eat his breakfast, she drove him to his preschool, walked him inside and kissed him. He seemed a little less nervous than he had been the previous week.

After she waved good bye, she returned to Rafe's house, full of restlessness. She still couldn't make sense of what had happened between her and Rafe last night, but she knew she couldn't blame him for it. She'd been an all-too-willing participant.

Her cell phone rang, distracting her from her thoughts. Her father's number appeared on the caller ID and her stomach tensed. She took a careful breath and answered.

"Hello, Father," she said in the calmest voice she could muster.

"Nicole, I've had a hard time getting in touch with you. I called your house with no response," her father said.

"That's because I'm not there," she said. "I decided Joel and I should take a little vacation. We're in Florida having a wonderful time."

"This is so sudden. You should have told me you were

going," he chided. "You know I like to keep tabs on you and my grandson."

The undertone of manipulation in his voice clawed across her skin like a scratchy sweater. "No need to worry," she said. "We're having a fabulous time. We're going to swim with the dolphins."

An uncomfortable silence followed. "Where exactly are you staying?" her father asked.

"Miami," she said. "In a cottage." The gross understatement stuck in her throat, but she swallowed it.

Another silence followed. "Miami," he echoed. "I have business contacts down there. I should visit."

Nicole felt a surge of panic. "Oh, I'm not sure about that. We're so busy. Joel is taking swimming lessons and we're doing kiddy activities every day."

"Hmmm," her father said.

Her nervousness rose with each passing second. "Well, I don't want to keep you," she said.

"You're not. I'm back from Greece. Working a deal with the Argyros cruise line. It looks promising. I should close it within the next week."

"Congratulations," she said, because she couldn't think of anything else.

"Good instincts and hard work," he said. "Let me talk to my grandson."

"He's in class at the moment," she said. "Art class."

"Art," he said with a condescending tone. "You need to get him into something more competitive. A man needs a competitive drive in this world."

"He's not a man yet," she said.

"But he will be. You need to make sure he's ready. I worry that you won't," he said with the slightest edge to his voice.

"No need to worry, Father. He's not quite four yet," she told him, tamping down her impatience.

"He's never too young to develop his competitive edge," he said.

"I hear you," she said, wanting to end the call, feeling as if he was closing in on her.

"You hear, but do you act?" he challenged.

"Of course, I do," she said. "Thank you for calling me. And congratulations on your new deal."

"I'll call again soon," he said, but his voice sounded like more of a threat than a comfort.

"Good-bye. Take care," she said and hung up. She stared at the phone, wishing she never had to speak to him again.

Talking with her father reminded her of unanswered questions about Rafe.

Nicole still wasn't content with the report from the private investigator. She wanted more information. Taking advantage of the time that Joel was in preschool, she drove to downtown Miami to visit Rafe's former employer. Although it was early in the day, the club also served lunch.

A young blonde woman, wearing a dress that show-cased her cleavage and long legs, greeted her. "How many for lunch?" she asked.

"I'd like to speak to the manager," Nicole said.

"Keno's hiring," the young woman said. "I'll see if he can talk to you now."

"But…" Nicole said to the woman's back. She'd already left.

A couple of moments later, the woman returned. "Come this way. Jerome has a few minutes since we're not busy."

"I'm not really—" She broke off as the woman led her

into an office that faced the white sands and turquoise water of South Beach.

A large, dark-skinned man nodded toward her. "You want a job? We need hostesses," he said and cocked his head to one side. "You're not bad, but you'll need more paint and shorter skirts. Have you considered going blonde?"

Nicole couldn't quite swallow a laugh at the man's suggestion. "My sister did that for me. I'm not here for a job. Are you Mr. Keno? I'm here to ask about Rafe Medici. I understand you were his employer several years ago."

He lifted an eyebrow. "Yes, I'm Mr. Keno. Why do you want to ask about Rafe?"

"Because he is the father of my sister's son," she said. "I need to know what kind of man Rafe really is."

"Why should I tell you?" he asked.

"Because you are a good, ethical man," she said with more hope than proof.

Jerome Keno laughed, revealing white teeth. "I've been called many things, but good and ethical are low on the list. You have a good cause, though, so I'll humor you. What concerns you about Rafe?"

"He was charged with battery while he worked for you," she said.

Keno shrugged. "Happens every now and then with bouncers. My lawyers always got the charges dismissed."

Nicole felt a shiver of fear. "Does that mean the charges weren't valid or your lawyer was good at his job?"

"Both," Keno said. "Rafe didn't use force unless it was absolutely necessary."

Still uneasy, Nicole bit the inside of her lip. "Would you say that he was an angry man? Did he have issues with his temper?"

"I never observed him to be out of control. If anything, he was extremely calculated when using physical force. Why are you asking?"

She resisted the urge to defend her concerns. The truth was she was afraid for Joel. "I want to make sure he wouldn't hurt a child. He's a passionate man. I don't want him to abuse his son."

Keno paused. "I don't believe he would ever use that anger against someone weaker than himself. His power lies in his self-control. That's only my opinion," he said. "My question for you is, what will you do when he learns that you have been investigating his past. Rafe has become a very powerful man."

"Rafe won't be surprised that I've investigated his past," she said. "He's done the same to me."

Keno shook his head and laughed. "Well, if you should need employment, give me a call. A short skirt and a different top... My customers would like you very much. So would I." he said.

Nicole left the club with less doubt than when she'd walked in, but she began to wonder if she would ever be able to fully trust Rafe. How much of that was Rafe's doing? How much of it went back to her father?

The next day, Tuesday, Rafe cleared his afternoon schedule in preparation for the visit from the social-services specialist. After lunch, he arrived home to find Nicole and Joel playing a board game with a woman who appeared to be in her late thirties.

Nicole glanced up at him. "Rafe, Joel and I have shown Mrs. Bell around the house and introduced her to the staff."

"Thanks," Rafe said and extended his hand to the woman. "Thank you for coming."

"It's good to meet you, Mr. Medici," Mrs. Bell said.

"Can we go to the pool now?" Joel asked, popping up from where he crouched on the floor.

"Sounds like a good plan to me," Rafe said.

"Cool!" Joel said, his eyes lighting up like blue sparklers. "I gotta get on my trunks."

Mrs. Bell smiled. "He must like the water."

"Oh, yeah," Rafe said with a surge of pride. "A regular fish. Of course, we have extra safeguards in place so he won't take any unsupervised swims."

"Excellent," Mrs. Bell said. "Nicole has mentioned the safety modifications throughout the house."

"Mom, come on, we gotta change clothes," Joel said, tugging at Nicole's hand.

"Excuse us. We'll be down in just a few minutes. Please have a seat by the pool," Rafe said. "I'll send my housekeeper out with something for you to drink."

Within minutes, Joel was leaping off the side of the pool into Rafe's arms. Chortling with glee, he clung to Rafe's back as he swam the length of the pool. Rafe noticed Nicole hadn't changed into her swimsuit and sat beside Mrs. Bell.

He wondered about her motive for staying out of the pool, but now wasn't the time to ask about it. After a while, he dragged a protesting Joel from the water to enjoy a snack the housekeeper brought poolside.

Afterward, Rafe noticed Joel rubbing his eyes. The little boy stood. "I wanna go back in the pool."

"You've had a busy day. You may need a little rest time," Rafe said.

"Don't wanna rest. I wanna go back in the pool."

"The pool will be here tomorrow. I don't want you to get too tired," Rafe said, rising. "Even fish get tired. I think

I'm going to catch a little fish who's wearing orange swim trunks and put him—"

Joel's eyes widened, then he squealed with laughter and ran in the opposite direction.

"Joel, don't run!" Rafe called. He took off after his son, reaching Joel just as he took a tumble on to the concrete patio.

Joel howled as his legs scraped against the concrete.

Rafe winced, immediately scooping up his son's little body. "Oh, buddy, I know that hurts."

"Mama," Joel wailed, his voice wavering with tears.

"You'll be okay," Rafe said. "Let me see—"

"Mama!" Joel screamed, his face contorting with pain. "I want Mama!"

Rafe felt an odd shot of helplessness as he scanned his son's skinned knees and shin.

Nicole rushed to his side and Joel immediately pitched himself toward her, wrapping himself around her as she took him into her arms. "Oh, sweetie, let's get some Band-Aids. This is why Rafe and I don't want you running around the pool."

Joel sobbed. "It hurts," he said.

"I know it does," she soothed. "But we'll make it stop." She glanced over her shoulder at Mrs. Bell with a wry smile. "Gravity can be a tough lesson for all of us," she said and carried Joel inside.

Mrs. Bell nodded and walked toward Rafe. "She's very important to him, isn't she?"

Rafe nodded, the incident underscoring what he already knew. "Yes, she is."

The meeting had been a disaster. A bitter taste filled his mouth. His frustration grew. He needed Nicole on his side. It was critical that he bring her around to his way of thinking.

Rafe plunged his fingers through his damp hair, nodding as Mrs. Bell made polite, neutral conversation. He pulled on his T-shirt. "I'll walk you to the door," he said and started to open the French doors to the den just as Nicole appeared with Joel in her arms, clutching a book.

"Hey," Rafe said, his heart twisting at the sight of his son. "How are ya?"

"I'm all better," Joel said solemnly. "I got Band-Aids," he said. "Dinosaur ones."

Rafe tousled Joel's hair. "Good for you."

"Mama said you might read a book to me on the patio if I asked you nice," Joel said.

"You bet I would," Rafe said, gazing at Nicole, feeling a well of gratitude and other emotions he couldn't name. He could tell she still wasn't sold on him, so this was a big step for her. He reached for Joel and his son clung to him.

After Joel was put to bed, Rafe and Nicole shared a quiet dinner. The tension between them was so thick she could feel it on her skin, in her lungs. She was keeping so many things from him, the fact that she'd had him investigated, her worries over her father. Exhausted from feeling like she was deceptive, she wondered if now was the time to tell him everything. She could feel him studying her with a mixture of curiosity and banked sexual need.

"So, why did you decide to make me look good?" he asked.

She choked on a sip of wine. "Dual goal," she said. "I wanted Joel to associate comfort and protection with you and I wanted Mrs. Bell to see that the two of you are building a relationship."

"That doesn't answer why," he said.

She bit her lip. "I want you to be a good father. I believe you can be."

The light in his dark eyes flared. He lifted his glass toward hers. "I will win over my son. What will it take to win over his mother?"

Her heart jolted in her chest.

"Mr. Medici," Carol said, saving Nicole from a response. "Miss Maddie Greene is here to see you."

Surprise and irritation crossed his face. "Send her in and bring a glass of wine for her."

"Red or white, sir?" the housekeeper asked.

"Red," Rafe said then turned to Nicole. "I have no idea why she came here tonight. I didn't request her presence."

"Maybe she wants to see you," Nicole said and swirled the wine in her glass. "Maybe her instincts tell her that another woman has encroached on her territory, even though I—"

"Maddie," he said, rising from his chair. "What a surprise. What could possibly be so important that you would come here at such a late hour?"

Maddie's face fell. "You and I conducted several business meetings after hours on the yacht," she said in a reproachful voice and glanced accusingly at Nicole.

"True," he said in a neutral tone. "What do you need?"

Maddie dragged her gaze back to Rafe's and seemed to force a smile. "It's not so much what I need as what you need. This contract needs to be signed and filed tomorrow," she said, sliding a set of papers in front of him.

"Has my attorney Jeff seen these?"

"Of course," Maddie said.

"Okay," Rafe said. "I'll look them over and bring them in tomorrow."

Maddie frowned. "But—"

"I always read whatever I sign," he reminded her.

She let out a long soft sigh. "Yes, of course." She cleared her throat. "We also received an envelope from Italy. I didn't open it because it was marked personal, but I thought you might want to see it," she said as she handed him the envelope.

Rafe took the envelope in his hand and studied it. "Emilia Medici," he said.

"A relative?" Nicole asked.

"Not one I've met, but she wrote me two other times. I wonder…" His cell phone rang, interrupting him. He glanced at his caller ID. "It's an international call. I should take it. Excuse me. I'll be back," he said and strode toward his downstairs office.

After he disappeared from view, Maddie picked up her glass of red wine and studied Nicole. "It's pretty nice here, isn't it? Living in a mansion with access to Rafe on a daily basis. I'm sure it's tempting to think something else could develop between you two. Especially since he was once crazy for your sister."

"Rafe is providing a home for his son. I'm just helping Joel and Rafe make some adjustments. If you'll excuse me." No longer hungry, she picked up her half-empty plate.

"Oh, don't rush off," Maddie said and pointed at Nicole's plate. "You haven't finished your dinner."

"I've had enough," Nicole said, thinking she meant that in more ways than one.

Maddie set down her wine glass and put her hand to her throat. "I didn't offend you, did I? I just know what kind of effect Rafe has on people, especially women. I would hate to see you get hurt. It would be easy for you to misinterpret the attention he pays you."

Nicole knew she should ignore the woman, but some

crazy part of her couldn't resist. "How would I misinterpret his attention?"

Maddie shot her a sympathetic glance. "Oh, no. He's already got you under his spell. Well, it's obvious that you're important to Rafe. You are the key to helping his son adjust, after all. Subconsciously he may think he can work through his latent desire for Tabitha," she said with a shrug then took another sip of her wine. "I'm sure he would never admit to such a thing. Too much pride."

Even though Nicole knew Maddie wanted Rafe for herself, she couldn't tamp down a flicker of self-doubt. Why had she made love with him? Why had she let down her guard? Heaven help her, he was getting to her.

"Back," Rafe said as he entered the room. "Thanks for bringing the contracts and the package from Italy. I know it was out of your way, so I won't keep you."

"Not at all," Maddie said, lighting up like the Fourth of July. "You know my first priority is my job as your assistant. Nothing is more important."

"Thanks," he said. "I'll walk you to the door."

Maddie slid a sideways glance at Nicole then returned her gaze to Rafe. "Thanks. Good night, Nicole," she said.

Just moments later, Rafe returned, but Nicole's emotions bubbled like a cauldron. She bit her lip to keep from saying anything about Maddie even though some part of her seethed with resentment. Although her relationship with Rafe was far from ideal, she had the odd feeling of having their little island contaminated after Maddie's visit. She would have to make sense of it later.

"That was an interruption I didn't expect. I'll have to tell her to give me warning in the future," Rafe said as he re-entered the dining area.

Nicole gave a noncommittal nod.

He glanced at the dining-room table. "You're finished eating?"

"I'm not hungry anymore. A full day," she said with a shrug.

"I'm not either," he said. "Let's go into the den. I wonder what Aunt Emilia has to say this time. She was my father's sister. Never married because her fiancé dumped her after the family lost the homeplace."

"That's terrible," she said, curious about the letter. She followed him into the den.

He sat down on the sofa and patted the seat beside him. "Do you want something to drink? I can ask the housekeeper."

"No, I'm good," she said, drawing in his scent and feeling a strange combination of arousal and something deeper. Something that bothered her.

He ripped open the envelope and a letter and three photos fell out. "Oh, my God," he muttered, picking up the photos.

Nicole had never seen Rafe so moved. He covered his mouth with one of his hands as he stared at the photos for a long time. She leaned over to look at them. "They're holding a baby," she said. "Your parents?"

He nodded. "That's me." He showed her another photo. "That's my brothers and me with my father."

Nicole lifted her fingers to the photos and couldn't help smiling. "You were a beautiful baby."

He gave a rough laugh then set down the pictures. "Let's see what crazy Aunt Emilia has to say. Dear Raphael: I am writing you because I know I'm not going to be around forever and I want you to have these photographs of yourself as a bambino. Your father sent me these when you were born and the latter photograph is from one of his last letters to me. He loved you, Damien, Michael and Leonardo very much. All of you have overcome so much. Damien in Las Vegas, you in Miami, Michael in Atlanta and Leonardo in Pennsylvania. I wish that I could have helped you after your father's death, but I am now thankful that all of you are doing so well. Congratulations on your son, Joel. I know that he and his mother will be a source of unbelievable joy to you. With much love, Emilia."

Rafe frowned at the letter. "How did she know about Joel? And what is this about Leo? Leo died in the same train accident as my father." He shook his head. "She must be confused."

"Is everything else correct?" Nicole asked.

"Yes, but—" He shook his head. "Leo in Pennsylvania. Hmmm." He looked at the photos again, his gaze hungry. "These are the only photos of my family. What I would give for more."

The intense emotion in his eyes grabbed at something inside her. Rafe had told her before how much he missed having photos from his family. The way he drank in the sight of those photos cut through her.

"You should make copies of those. You wouldn't want to lose them."

He shook his head vehemently. "I'll scan them, too." He paused. "You have no idea how many nights I spent wishing for just one photograph of my parents. After they died and my brothers and I were divided up, it was as if my foster family wanted to pretend my other family never existed. After a while, it became like a dream. With no photographs, I had no proof."

Nicole felt her eyes sting with tears, her throat knot into

a well of emotion. "I have something I'd like to give you," she said. "I'll be back in a couple of moments."

Gnawing on her lip, she climbed the stairs and checked on Joel before she went to her suite.

She turned on her laptop and reviewed the report the P.I. had sent her. The assault charges still made her heart stutter, but she realized that Rafe had a good explanation.

She continued through the pdf file and looked at the newspaper article reporting the death of Anthony Medici. A photograph of the Medici family accompanied the article. In it, she saw four boys with dark curly hair standing in front of a tall dark-haired man and a slim woman. She wondered if Rafe even knew this photo existed.

Eyeing the printer on the desk, she printed off the photo and trimmed away the article describing his family tragedy. She took the photo downstairs and gave it to him. He studied the photograph in surprise, then met her gaze.

"Where did you find this?" he asked in a low voice.

She crossed her arms under her chest. "That's a rather involved story for this time of night."

"I'm not sleeping and neither are you," he said, standing and resting one of his hands on his hip.

She dreaded telling him where she'd found the photo, but knew it had to be done. "Do you remember how you paid a P.I. to do a background check on me?"

"Yeah," he said, studying her and nodding in understanding. "You did the same to me. Learn anything interesting?"

"It mostly just confirmed everything you've told me," she said, resisting a sudden urge to fidget.

"It's late, so let's not beat around the bush. What bothered you? That I didn't graduate from an Ivy League school? That my family didn't come over on the Mayflower?"

"The assault charges," she said, tired of hiding her worries.

Realization crossed his face. "From my bouncer days. Yeah. I told you it was my job to escort out-of-control customers from the premises. Unfortunately, by the time they got out of control, they didn't go willingly. The charges were all dropped," he said.

"Right," she said, wishing that was enough to calm all her fears. "But Tabitha told me you were a bully. She said you were controlling."

"You keep saying that." He tilted his head as he studied her. "She didn't tell you that I hit her, did she? I've never touched a woman that way. What the hell else did she tell you?"

"She didn't say you hit her, but she kept calling you a bully," she said.

"That's what all these questions about assault have been about all along, right?" he asked, his voice filled with bitterness.

"I had to make sure you wouldn't hurt Joel. I had to protect him. She said you were like our father," she finally said.

He shrugged. "What does that mean? The only thing I know about your father is that he's a snob and a successful businessman. I'm no snob, but I've done well with my business."

"My father abused us," she said, unable to keep it in any longer. "That's why I avoid him. It's why my mother left him. She got a huge settlement if she agreed not to reveal how many times he'd slapped her. Tabitha was much better at playing him than I was. He hit her a few times, but most of the time I was the target."

He stared at her. "Your father did that? He beat you?" he asked.

Her heart twisted at the disbelief in his voice. "Don't ask me to prove it. You don't have to believe me, but it's true. That's why I had to make sure you wouldn't hurt Joel. I would do anything to make sure that didn't happen to him."

He met her gaze. "I believe you. I'm not a violent man, but I would like to beat the crap out of him for touching a hair on your head."

She took a deep breath and felt a sinking sense of relief. "So, now, maybe you understand why I want to make sure that you won't harm Joel."

"I would never," he said, moving toward her. "And I would never harm you. I can't promise, however, that I wouldn't hurt someone who threatened Joel or you."

She took another breath. "Hopefully that won't happen."

He lifted her hand to his mouth. "I wish I knew why your sister lied about me."

Distracted by his touch, Nicole tried to summon a reason for Tabitha's actions. "I don't know," she whispered. "I wish I knew, too."

"She was wild when I first met her. I caught her taking some pills one time when we first started seeing each other. I made her swear she would stop. I thought I would be a stabilizing influence. I asked her to marry me. I thought I could help turn her around," he said.

Although Tabitha had kept her drug usage secret, Nicole had suspected that her sister had dabbled in drugs. After Joel had been born, she'd held her breath in hopes that he hadn't been affected.

"I always thought she was the stronger one," she said. "When we were growing up, she would challenge my father for anything."

"He didn't abuse her?" he asked.

"Very rarely, but she somehow was able to dance around his anger. I still don't know how she did it," Nicole said.

"But you took the brunt of it," he concluded, his voice full of disgust.

"I don't know why. I tried to be invisible, but it didn't work. I was always so relieved to go back to boarding school so I could be away from him." She glanced at him. "I don't want you to think I'm ungrateful."

He looked at her, perplexed. "Ungrateful?"

"I was very fortunate that my parents were wealthy enough to send me to the best schools. I received health care and education."

"You were also abused. You didn't deserve that."

"I have to keep reminding myself of that fact."

"I'll remind you," he said, moving closer to her, taking her into his arms.

Nicole slumped against him, inhaling his strength. She gave in to the urge to lift her hands to his hair and savored the sensation of his crisp hair in her fingers.

"This isn't wise," she said, but couldn't stop herself from leaning against him.

"I disagree," he said. "It feels right," he said and dipped his head, taking her mouth with his.

Nicole clung to him, wishing she could inhale all of him, all of his strength so that she would never feel weak or vulnerable again.

"I want to stay with you tonight," he muttered against her throat.

He heart quickened. "Rafe," she said, torn in different directions.

"Tell me you don't want me to stay," he whispered. "Tell me you don't want me."

"I do," she said, but forced herself to step away from him. She didn't want to confuse Joel if—when Rafe lost interest in her. "But being with you is just going to make things more complicated. We can't do this."

Nine

Rafe picked up his brother Michael at the private airport. "Nice surprise," he said as his brother crammed his backpack into the non-existent backseat of Rafe's Corvette.

"Thanks for picking me up," Michael said. "I would normally just take a morning flight, but this guy wanted to meet at 8 a.m. and I didn't trust the airlines or the private jet service in winter."

"It's not winter here," Rafe said, shifting gears and pulling away from the terminal.

Michael chuckled. "Rub it in. How's your son? How's Nicole?"

"Joel is great. Nicole needs some work," Rafe said, unable to keep a growl from his voice. He decided to wait to tell Michael about Aunt Emilia's letter when he could show him the photographs. "Tell me about the business deal that would drag you from Atlanta so you could have an o'dark-thirty meeting in Miami."

Michael discussed the deal and twenty minutes later, Rafe pulled into the garage.

"Nice crib," Michael said.

"Back side is better," Rafe said with a smile. "Come inside little brother."

Michael rolled his eyes. "Yeah, yeah."

Leading his brother through the garage, Rafe opened the side door and heard Joel squeal.

"He's home!"

Rafe couldn't stop the joy that filled him. "Where's my man?" he called, and Joel came running.

"Joel, you're wet," Nicole called. "Let me dry you—"

Joel skidded toward him as if the wooden floor were a Slip-n-Slide. Rafe rushed toward the boy and picked him up so he wouldn't get hurt. "Hey, you need to dry off those feet, or you could get in trouble."

Joel just beamed. "I been swimming. I can go from one side of the pool to the other."

Rafe grinned at his son. "Good for you. Do you remember your Uncle Michael from Atlanta?"

"We met just before you left."

Joel looked at Michael with a blank expression on his face.

Michael laughed. "No problem, guy. Next time I'll bring a gift."

Nicole appeared breathlessly. "Not necessary. He's not at all deprived."

Rafe looked Nicole over from head to toe. She wore a black bikini that made him want to strip it off. "Looks like the two of you have been having fun," he said.

She nodded and turned to Michael. "Please forgive my appearance. I didn't know we were having guests."

"Nothing to forgive," Michael said. "You should always dress this way for guests. It will leave all of us nearly speechless."

Rafe tossed his brother a quelling glance. "I'll get Carol to show you to your room."

"But I'm enjoying this show much more," Michael protested.

"Carol," Rafe called, feeling protective.

His housekeeper immediately appeared. "Yes, sir."

"Please show my brother to the blue guest room."

"Yes, sir. Welcome home," she said.

"Thank you," he replied.

"Such a grouch," Michael said, but allowed himself to be led away.

Nicole grabbed towels for Joel and herself.

"I petted a frog," Joel announced.

"You did?" Rafe said, wrapping the towel around his son and pulling him up into his arms. "How did he feel?"

"He was slippery. Frogs are cool. I like the way they croak," Joel said. "My teacher said we get turtles next week."

"You like school?"

Joel nodded. "It's fun. And I like the pool here."

Rafe glanced at Nicole in triumph, but glimpsed a shadow of pain and uncertainty in her eyes. It stopped him. "Are you okay?"

"Of course," she said, but the words sounded forced. "I should get Joel into a bath and then to bed."

"I can help," he said.

She looked as if she intended to protest, then closed her mouth. "That would be great," she said and led Joel upstairs.

Rafe followed after her, unable to keep his gaze from her round derriere. He remembered grasping her hips as he thrust inside… Growing hard at the memory, he reined in his need. He would have her again. It was just a matter of time.

He helped Joel with bath time and after Nicole dressed him in snuggly pajamas, Rafe read two books. Joel fell asleep before Rafe finished the second story and he left his son's room to go downstairs.

He found Nicole and Michael eating dishes of ice cream at the bar. Out of nowhere, he felt a sharp stab of jealousy. Her hair damp from a shower, Nicole wore shorts that revealed her long, lithe legs and a tank top.

"How did I miss the ice cream party?" he asked, keeping his tone light.

"I wandered into the kitchen and found Nicole with ice cream," Michael said. "Couldn't resist."

Yeah, right, Rafe thought. "Is there any left?"

"I can share," Nicole said, offering him her spoon and he felt just a bit mollified.

She lifted her spoon and he covered her hand with his and swallowed the bite of intensely chocolate ice cream. "Good," he said.

She smiled. "I put it on the shopping list. A forbidden indulgence."

"I'll take another," he said.

She lifted another spoonful to his mouth and he slid his tongue over the cold creamy confection then sucked it down his throat. He saw her eyes darken with sensual awareness.

Michael coughed. "Nicole told me you received a letter with photos from Aunt Emilia?"

Rafe nodded. "I got a copy made for you," he said,

reaching for his briefcase. He'd viewed the photos several times during the day, and each time was filled with bitter-sweet emotions. "It was so long ago it almost felt like pretend. A dream. This makes it more real," he said, still surprised at the comfort the photos brought him.

Michael glanced over his shoulder. "Look. Damien's hair is sticking straight up in that one."

Although his chest felt tight, Rafe nodded and managed a laugh. "And Leo's lifting his chin like he's gunning for a fight." He studied the faces of his mother and father. "I remember thinking Dad was so strong, never needing rest, but they both look tired."

"What do you expect when they had to take care of four hellions like us?" Michael asked.

"The letter was strange. I'll let you take a look at it. Emilia said that Leonardo isn't dead. She said something about him being successful in Pennsylvania."

Rafe looked at Michael and saw his brother's face turn pale.

"Where is she? Where is this woman? I need to talk to her," Michael said.

Rafe shook his head. "I ran a search for a phone number from the return address, but they said she had worked as a caretaker for their children. She moved on to take another job and left no forwarding address. I'm going to put an investigator on it."

"He couldn't be alive," Michael said to Rafe. "Could he?"

Rafe knew Michael had felt guilt for Leonardo's death. After all, Michael had gotten in trouble, so Leonardo had taken his place on that fateful trip on the train to the baseball game so many years ago.

"Don't get your hopes up," he cautioned Michael.

"But she had pictures," Nicole said. "Pictures of all of you. And she knew about Joel," she said to Rafe.

"Easy to say, now that he's here," Rafe said.

"I know it's strange, but—"

"Damn right it's strange," Rafe said. "We're already tracking Leo. I intend to check her out, too. She could answer a lot of questions about our past. Maybe the time has come for us to get those answers."

Ten

Rafe's cell phone rang. He took the business call from one of his clients and left Michael with Nicole on the patio.

"It's good of you to help Rafe through this adjustment period with Joel," Michael said to Nicole. "Learning that he had a son knocked him sideways. Of course, he recovered because that's what he does."

"I'm not sure how much help he's needed. I'm getting the impression that all the Medici brothers are quite resilient," she said, glimpsing some of the same drive in Michael that she saw in Rafe. Michael came across as quieter and more solemn.

Michael nodded. "Necessary for survival."

"But all of you have done more than survive. You're all very successful."

"True. I think it's partly a control issue," he said and gave a slight smile. "Never want to be poor, never want to be at the mercy of someone else, never want to care too much that losing something or someone will blow our world apart." He shrugged. "That one has gone by the wayside for Damien and Rafe. Damien fell in love and got married and now Rafe has a son he would give his life for."

"Is Damien more like you or Rafe?"

"Damien is me times ten," Michael said. "He used to be described as the terminator because he never let his emotions affect his decisions. Rafe hides his wounds with a joke. I remember when we were kids, he stepped on a nail and tore up his foot. My parents didn't take him to the doctor until the next day because he kept saying it wasn't that bad."

"So, he was like that even before your family was split up," Nicole mused, and even though she'd heard the story of what had happened to the Medicis before, the horror of it hit her again. "Rafe's been so determined for Joel to know that he has a father and that his father will always be there for him. I know the loss was terrible, but Rafe comes across as so strong. He's so confident, it's almost—"

"Frightening?" Michael finished for her. "You look beneath the surface. You won't underestimate him."

"My sister did," she said, and wondered if Tabitha had been afraid of Rafe because of his raw power.

"I think you're smarter than that," he said.

She laughed and shook her head. "Smart enough to know I'm not the right woman to handle that man."

"What makes you say that?"

"He needs a woman who can stand toe-to-toe with him and look him in the eye without flinching. Plus, most powerful men aren't satisfied with just one woman," she said.

Michael wore an odd expression on his face and looked just beyond her shoulder.

"The things I learn when I leave my younger brother with the lady of the house," Rafe said and Nicole felt a wave of embarrassment mixed with frustration.

"I'm not the lady of the house," she said.

"I don't see any other ladies around here except those who are employed to work here. I don't know whether to be flattered or insulted," Rafe said. "You not only know what kind of woman I need, you accuse me of running around on my future wife before I've even made it down the aisle."

"I didn't say you, specifically. I said most powerful men. In my previous life, I saw the inner workings of a lot of those power marriages, and trust me there was definitely a shortage of love and loyalty."

"Sounds like you might be a little prejudiced when it comes to successful men," he said lightly, but his gaze held hers.

"Again, I didn't say successful. I said powerful. There's a difference. With everything I've learned, I came to the conclusion a long time ago that if I ever marry, it will be to an ordinary man."

Michael chuckled.

Rafe dipped his head, but his eyes were full of challenge. "You may have a tough time pulling that off given the fact that you are not an ordinary woman."

"You're full of flattery, but I see straight through it," she said.

"Michael," he said, "tell me, would you call Nicole an ordinary woman?"

"Not in a million years," Michael said.

"She looks like she would be sweet and demure," Rafe said. "That wealthy upbringing and those classy manners. Then she opens her mouth."

"You don't have to talk about me as if I'm not here," she said, feeling heat rise to her cheeks. Damn it if the man didn't make her feel more alive than she'd felt in years. She just wasn't sure she loved or hated the feeling.

"Handful," Rafe said. "Definitely a handful."

Unable to bear another moment under his seductive and challenging gaze, she lifted her hands. "I'm going to bed. You two deserve each other."

"Giving up so easily?" Rafe called after her.

"To quote your brother," she said over her shoulder. "Not in a million years."

"You're right," Michael said after Nicole left the room. "She's a handful. What do you have planned for her?"

Rafe glanced at his brother. "I'm going to marry her."

Michael's eyes widened. "Whoa, that's fast."

Rafe shrugged and took a swallow from his bottle of Corona. "It may take longer than I want, but it will happen."

"Does she know this?"

"She will soon enough."

"I see some sparks between you, old man, but I'm not sure she's sold," Michael said with more than a trace of doubt. "She doesn't seem all that impressed with your success."

"She isn't," Rafe said, narrowing his eyes. "But that doesn't matter. What matters is that she is Joel's mother and I am his father and we *will* be a family. I won't have Joel's life torn up like mine was. She'll come around."

Silence followed. "Pardon my ignorance, but I didn't hear anything in that plan that includes romance, let alone love. I hear most ladies want one or the other, if not both."

Rafe shrugged. "I went head over butt over Nicole's sister. I acted like a fool. I did my lust/love time. I'm not doing it again. Nicole will come around because she has Joel's best interests at heart. Joel is the most important person in the world to her. She will see that marriage between us is the best thing for Joel."

"Hmmm," Michael said, his tone noncommittal.

His brother's lack of confidence in Rafe's plan grated on him. "What? You don't think I can make this happen?"

"Maybe," Michael said. "I just don't think this woman is going to commit to you so easily. She seems like she has an ax to grind with super-successful men. Add to the fact that you're not going to do anything to romance her or even pretend that you love her, and I'm not sure you can pull it off, bro. Not even with all your charm, and heaven knows you got the lion's share of it among the brothers."

"Don't be surprised when I call to tell you I'm hitched," Rafe said.

"Whatever," Michael said, clearly still unconvinced. "So, what do you think about our Auntie from Italy? Do you think she's legit?" Michael paused for a long moment. "Can you imagine if Leo were alive?" he asked, his voice full of a bone-deep wish borne of too many sleepless nights to count.

Rafe felt a stab of sympathy for his brother. Michael had suffered from guilt over Leo's death for most of his life.

"Like I said before, Michael, I wouldn't count on it."

"If he is, I'll find him," Michael said, the hope dimming in his eyes, but still there.

"Yeah. It's a long shot, but I'll look into it from my end, too," he said.

"It was a long shot that you would be as successful as you are," Michael said.

"Yeah," Rafe agreed. "I guess almost anything is possible."

"Good luck convincing Nicole of that," Michael said.

Rafe gave him a fake punch. "Don't give me a hard time. She's doing a good enough job for three of you."

On Saturday morning, Rafe took care of business from home, worked out and was sipping a cup of coffee as he read *The Wall Street Journal* when Nicole and Joel came down the steps. He glanced up to find the two of them dressed almost identically—jeans, T-shirts and tennis shoes.

Spotting a gleam of purpose in both their gazes, he felt an odd pinch of disappointment because he'd decided the three of them could take another cruise this afternoon.

"You look like you two have plans," Rafe said.

Joel gave a big solemn nod. "We got something important to do. After we eat breakfast, we're giving soup away."

Rafe did a double take and met Nicole's gaze. "Soup?"

She nodded, pride emanating from her. "Yes. Joel and I are going to help at a soup kitchen today. We volunteered in Atlanta and we're doing the same here in Miami."

"Why didn't you tell me? I could have donated enough soup for the kitchen for several months, if not a year," Rafe said.

"It's not about money," she said. "It's about service. Taking action. Giving of yourself."

"Oh," he said, seeing that she was trying to teach Joel a different lesson. He also saw that Joel seemed quite proud of the fact that he was participating in the endeavor. Rafe felt a surprising spike of his own pride. He put aside his newspaper. "Well, hell, I'll join you."

Nicole blinked. "You will?"

"Sure," he said. "Why not? It's just giving soup to people. I can do that."

"True, but you have to respect them," she said.

"Respect?" he echoed, pointing to his chest. "I can give respect."

"Okay," she said. "Can we skip using your chauffeur this time?"

He chuckled. "Embarrassed by my wealth?" he asked and shook his head. This was a first and he kinda liked it.

Two hours later, he felt his perspective turned ninety degrees. He served soup to a former CEO, a homeless woman and a dozen children. Rafe had always dedicated a generous amount of his income to charity, but this visit to the soup kitchen made him feel his contribution had been paltry.

At the same time, he couldn't help but admire Nicole's empathetic nature and Joel's industriousness. He saw the joy Joel brought to both the adults and the other children and felt a swell of pride.

Afterward, he drove the three of them to an ice cream shop. "You were good, Joel," he said. "Give me a high five."

Joel lifted his hand and Rafe gently slapped it. "You did good, too," Joel said. "Since it was your first time."

Rafe heard Nicole unsuccessfully swallow a snicker and glanced up at her. "What?" he asked. "I don't serve soup on a daily basis."

"You just need some practice," Joel said. "Daddy," he added.

Rafe's heart twisted in his chest, and he pulled Joel against him. "Yeah, I need some practice at a lot of things."

Out of the corner of his gaze, he saw Nicole rub one of her eyes before she pulled her sunglasses on to her nose. "I'd say you're doing pretty good," she murmured.

"High praise from you," he said. "You've got tough standards."

She shrugged. "Being an instant single father has got to be tough."

"I don't feel single," he said, allowing Joel to step away and eat his ice cream. "I feel like I have an expert partner."

Her mouth stretched into a grin and she gave a low laugh. "I haven't given you Daddy lessons in a while. It's time for lesson number two. There are no expert parents. We're all amateurs doing the best we can."

He met her gaze and felt a dipping sensation in his gut. Nicole touched him and challenged him on more levels than any woman ever had. Oddly enough, Rafe had the sense she'd only scratched the surface of how she could impact him.

"If that's lesson number two, then what's lesson number one?"

"Just love 'em," she said.

"I'm listening, teacher."

She looked into his eyes and he felt a strange zing that mixed with a longing deep inside him. What would it take to get Nicole to marry him?

Hours later, after the three spent the later afternoon in the pool and enjoying a barbecue dinner, Nicole had retreated to her bedroom. Rafe had noticed she'd been distracted several times throughout the evening.

He'd also noticed that she'd frowned when she'd looked at her cell phone.

That didn't stop her from helping to put Joel to bed, but she'd disappeared to her room before Rafe could question her. Unable to sleep, he worked on an international expansion plan for his business. He finally grew drowsy and went to bed.

Nicole's screams awakened him. He sat upright in bed and raced toward her room.

She tossed and turned, struggling with sheets and some unnamed demon. "No, no. You can't have him. You'll ruin him."

He eased his hand over her shoulder. "Nicole, you're dreaming."

"No. I won't let you take him."

Frowning at her words, he gently nudged her. "Nicole, sweetheart, you need to wake up."

She shook her head then blinked her eyes. Seconds passed when he could tell that she struggled for consciousness. She took several shallow breaths.

"Rafe?"

"Yeah, it's me."

She took another breath. "It was my father. He called again and left a message on my phone. He's trying to get Joel."

Alarm shot through him. "What? Was this a dream?"

She shook her head and licked her lips as if they were dry from fear. "No. He's always wanted Joel. I couldn't let him have Joel. He would have destroyed him."

"Nicole, are you sure of what you're telling me? Is your father trying to take Joel away?"

She closed her eyes. "He always wanted Joel, but since I refused his support, he couldn't take him. He's always watching me, waiting for the day when I weaken or fail."

Rafe swore under his breath. "And you've been living with this since Tabitha died?"

She nodded. "He called over a week ago. He wanted to come down to visit. I think the only thing that kept him away was some deal he was working with someone in Greece."

Rafe narrowed his eyes. "Argyros," he said.

She nodded. "That sounds right." She opened her eyes. "He left a message on my phone today, telling me he insists on coming down for a visit. I can't let him take Joel."

"There's a solution," he said.

"What?"

"Marry me."

Eleven

Nicole tried to keep up with her galloping heart. "How would that solve anything?"

Rafe shrugged. "Even with all your father's money and influence, he wouldn't stand a chance against you and me together," he said, a tinge of bitterness sharpening his voice.

She met his gaze. "But how can I be sure?" she asked. "How can I be sure that you will be good to Joel?"

"How have you seen me act so far? What's the evidence? If being devoted to my son were a crime, would I be convicted?" he asked.

His fervent response stabbed at her heart. He was right. Rafe may not have stepped into fatherhood shoes perfectly, but he'd done it with passion and gentleness. She couldn't deny that truth. "Okay," she said and knew she was about to take a huge leap. "How do we do this? When?"

"As soon as possible," he said. "I'll make the arrangements."

* * *

On Monday morning, Rafe took Nicole to the county courthouse to obtain the marriage license. In exchange for the presentation of their photo IDs and eighty-six dollars and fifty cents, they were given a sixteen-page booklet, which pretty much provided a bounty of reasons why a man or woman would run screaming from the institution of marriage.

Rafe barely resisted the urge to snag the document from Nicole.

"This could be a huge mistake," she said, flipping through the pages.

'It's full of worst-case scenarios," he said, reaching over to cup her knee in reassurance. "You and I are intelligent adults. We share the same goal."

"Division of assets," she said. "Spousal abuse. I think I'm going to be sick."

"I will never *abuse* you or Joel." He tightened his grip on the steering wheel. "I can't promise what I'll do if your father even hints of threatening you or Joel, but I'll keep you safe. I swear it."

She took a deep breath. "Part of me believes you, but your size is intimidating."

"Would you rather I be weak? Don't tell me you find an out-of-shape guy more attractive?"

He caught her shooting him a sideways glance and a reluctant smile. "I didn't say that. I just—" She broke off. "Your strength is both comforting and intimidating."

"And a turn-on," he said.

She sucked in a quick breath. "I didn't say that."

"But it is."

"That could sound cocky," she told him.

"But it doesn't," he said.

"Because it's true." She paused. "We haven't discussed how this marriage is going to work. Do you expect monogamy?"

"Yes," he said before she finished.

He felt her gaze on his face. "Better be careful not to promise to do something you can't," she said.

Surprised at her comment, he pulled into a parking lot. "What are you saying? That I expect more from you than I'm willing to give of myself."

She chewed on her lip, but continued to meet his gaze. "I grew up with a man who was wealthy and powerful. He felt that the reciprocal rules of monogamy didn't apply to him. I also know that many women consider wealth and power an aphrodisiac. There's a lot of temptation out there."

He nodded, unable to keep his cynicism in check. "Are we talking about your father or about me?"

Her eyes flashed with a half dozen emotions. "There was a time when you wanted Tabitha. I'm not—and never will be her."

Rafe lowered his head and took her mouth in a brief, but firm kiss. "Good."

Over the next twenty-four hours, Nicole doubted herself and Rafe every other moment. Had she lost her mind?

When she calmed down enough to think it through, however, she believed in her heart that Rafe only wanted to do what was best for Joel. She could tell that he loved his son and was devoted to him.

Rafe's relationship with her, however, was a different story. He might want her, but he wasn't crazy for her. The reality hurt. It shouldn't, but it did. She wanted him to love her like no other. Why? Because, despite her best efforts, she had fallen for him.

Heaven help her if he never gave his heart to her. She would spend an eternity wanting more than he could give. She could only hope that somewhere along the way, he would also fall for her.

The next day, she dressed for her so-called marriage. On a whim, she'd gone shopping while Joel had been in pre-school. She'd found a cream-silk-colored, empire-waist tank dress that flirted with the tops of her knees. She'd purchased a cream, lace purse and wore the pearls her mother had given her when she'd turned eighteen.

When Nicole looked in the mirror, she almost didn't recognize herself. She looked like a confident, modern bride. Only she knew how full of doubt she truly was.

Gathering her composure, she walked down the stairs and met Rafe at the bottom landing. He wore a black suit and red tie. His white shirt contrasted with his tanned skin, dark hair and eyes.

He extended his hand. "You look beautiful."

"Thank you," she said, then smiled. "So do you."

He lifted his hand, skimming it through her hair. "You really are beautiful."

"Are you sure you don't wish I were blonde?" she asked, thinking of Tabitha.

"Absolutely sure," he said and lifted her hand to his mouth. "Let's get this show on the road."

Nicole slid into the limo and for the first time in her life wanted a double martini before noon. Was this the right thing to do? Ultimately for Joel, she believed it was. But for her?

Rafe had offered her a generous prenuptial agreement with the understanding that they would make every possible effort to remain together. The agreement also included the provision that she would retain dual custody of Joel if they should separate. Deep inside, she knew that such a situation would kill Rafe. He was determined to create a safe and happy environment for Joel.

Again, she wondered what was *her* future? What if Rafe never felt anything more for her than a convenient sort of passion? Her stomach knotted at the thought.

Before she knew it, the chauffeur parked the limo and she and Rafe entered the court building. In front of a magistrate, she promised and he promised. In the sterile surroundings, he lowered his mouth to hers in a kiss that stood for an oath of a lifetime.

Nicole stared into his dark eyes, praying she hadn't made a mistake. He took her hand and didn't let go, even as he led her outside. "Where do you want to eat?"

She swallowed over the lump in her throat. "I haven't even thought about it."

He met her gaze. "Think about it now. What fast food do you want to eat to celebrate our marriage?"

Her heart skipped a beat and she took a deep breath. "Some sort of terrible cheeseburger with extra mustard and pickles. Greasy French fries. Something chocolate."

He nodded. "I've got just what you want."

He had no idea, she thought, how much she wanted him.

A half hour later, they ate greasy cheeseburgers, fries, ice cream and champagne in the back of the limo.

"This has got to be one of the worst possible gastronomic combinations," she said, taking a drink of champagne and following with a spoonful of ice cream.

He clinked his glass against hers. "Tastes good going down," he said and swallowed a glass of bubbly in two gulps.

Nicole's head was spinning. "But will we pay in the morning?"

"Maybe," he said. "I say if we're going to get a hangover, then let's make it worth the pain."

He lowered his mouth to hers and her head spun even more. His kiss heated her from the inside out.

"You're so cool then you're hot," he muttered against her mouth. "I spend too much time wanting to make you as hot as I feel."

He slipped one of his hands over her breast, the other beneath the hem of her silk dress. She gasped at the heat that rolled through her like lava from a volcano.

"Rafe," she whispered.

"You're my wife," he said, rubbing his mouth against her cheek then lower against her throat. "We're married. We may as well make the most of it."

He was now her husband, her man. The knowledge unleashed something primitive inside her. Arching against him, she didn't fight when he slid her dress up over her hips and pushed her panties down her legs. The world seemed to spin around her. She thrust her fingers through his hair, steeping herself in his strength and passion.

His kisses sent her into another galaxy where only he existed. His erection thrust inside her intimately, taking her. Shocking herself with need, she craved being taken. The rhythm took her up and over to heights she'd never experienced.

"Rafe," she whispered, clinging to him.

"Nicole," he muttered, flying into his own climax. "You're mine. All mine."

A half hour later, they pulled into the drive of his house. Rafe's eyes were lowered to a sexy half-mast.

"We *will* have a honeymoon," he said. "Just later." He took her mouth in a sensual kiss. "Damn, I'd like it to be now."

"We don't want to leave Joel yet," she said.

"I agree," he said, sliding his hands through her hair and taking her mouth again. "Just keep reminding me."

She could almost believe that he wanted *her*, not just because she was Joel's mother. "There's so much I don't know about you."

"You'll learn," he said. "And so will I." He sighed. "The mother's helper took Joel to preschool, right?"

She nodded.

"I hate it, but I need to do a little business," Rafe said. "We can meet again after dinner."

"Okay," she said. "In the den?"

"No," he said, his gaze dark with sexy possessiveness. "You're my wife. You'll sleep in my suite now."

That afternoon she rode with the chauffeur to pick up Joel after preschool. Rafe, Nicole and Joel shared a barbecue prepared by the chef for dinner. Steak for Rafe and Nicole, hamburger for Joel. Tired from his active day, Joel took an early bedtime.

Rafe took advantage and led Nicole to his big bed. "I've wanted you since I met you," he whispered, removing her clothes from her body.

He made her feel sexy and sensual, forbidden and powerful. "I'll do whatever it takes to make you and Joel happy," he said, sliding his mouth down over her throat and breasts and lower down her abdomen.

Nicole's breath caught in her throat. She'd never felt so sensual and sexy in her life, but she couldn't help wondering if she was a means to an end. She tried to push the doubt aside.

She felt him lower his mouth to take her femininity and her mind scrambled. "Rafe."

"Let me have you," he urged. "In every way."

His mouth took her to a level she'd never been, sending her into spasms of pleasure. Rising upward, he plunged inside her again and she felt herself tighten around him. His gasp of pleasure took her over the top again.

"More," he muttered, climaxing inside her. "Can't get enough of you."

She embraced him intimately and slid her fingers through his hair. She understood. She couldn't get close enough. Sliding her legs around his waist, she embraced him. She wanted more of him. She wanted everything. But would he give himself to her the same way she gave herself to him?

Rafe had never felt better in his life. He awakened the next morning with Nicole naked in his arms. His first instinct was to roll over and slide inside her, but he restrained himself.

Best to give his new bride a chance to adjust, although she'd done a damn good job of taking him to Neverland last night.

He luxuriated in the sensation of her naked skin against his. Her breasts meshed with his chest, her thighs twined through his. Her cheek nuzzled against his throat.

He could take her again at this second. The only thing that kept him was that she was his bride. Since Tabitha, he'd never believed he would get married, but Nicole had changed his mind.

She thought he only wanted her because of Joel, but that was wrong. He wanted her in every sense of the word. He wanted her because she made him feel things he'd never thought he could feel. She reminded him of things about himself he'd forgotten. She made him feel cherished and needed. She made him feel as if he wanted to step up and meet her needs, Joel's needs.

"Good morning," she said. Her eyes fluttered open and she dipped her head, sighing against his bare skin. The sensation was soft and sensual.

"Good morning," he murmured. He trailed his fingers down the sides of her breasts, groaning as she rubbed against him.

She lifted her hands to his shoulders, tracing the contours of his muscles all the way down his arms to his hands. Then she stroked his chest and lower with a feminine curiosity that made him hard.

"I thought I would give you a break," he said, groaning again as her hand barely skimmed his erection.

"Why would you do that?" she asked.

Unable to resist the sexual challenge in her gaze, he rolled on to his back and pulled her on top of him.

Her eyes widened in surprise, but two heartbeats later, she rose and slowly lowered herself on to him, encasing him in her moist femininity.

He'd known there was a fire underneath her cool composure, but he hadn't suspected the siren who would take his breath away as she began to ride him. Her breasts rubbed against his chest and she lowered her mouth to his. He suckled her tongue into his mouth and quickly felt himself pushed to the edge, but he held back until her body clenched and shuddered in release.

"Can't get enough of you, Nicole," he said, and finally allowed himself to climax.

* * *

The following morning, Nicole awakened, dimly recalling Rafe's kiss before he left her. It almost seemed like a dream, but her lips were swollen and her body ached in secret, sensitive places.

"Mommy, wake up," Joel said, bouncing up and down on Rafe's bed.

"Look at you," she said, smiling at his enthusiasm. "What is happening at preschool today?"

"Turtles," he said, looking at her as if she should have remembered. "We get to pet turtles. Can I bring one home?"

"Not today," she said, ruffling his curly hair. "But I want you to give me a report on turtles."

"Are we gonna get one?" Joel asked, bouncing up and down.

She tapped his little nose with her finger. "We'll see. We need to do some research. Now scoot so I can take a quick shower."

An hour later, she took Joel to school, then returned home. Just as she was entering the house, she overheard the chauffeur, Dan, talking to Carol.

"I'll have to cancel the repair for the limo. Mr. Medici called and he needs me to bring an envelope from his home office."

"I can do it," she offered. Rafe had extended an open invitation for her to visit him when he was working on the yacht. She knew he would be busy, but she would be satisfied just to see him for a few moments. The last couple of days had felt like a dream. Even though she wore the diamond band he'd placed on her finger, their marriage still felt surreal.

"That's very nice of you Miss—" The chauffeur broke off and smiled. "Mrs. Medici, but not necessary."

Hearing the man refer to her as Mrs. Medici took her off guard. "It's okay," she said. "It's really no trouble. I didn't have anything else planned."

"If you're sure," he said. "Mr. Medici said the envelope was on his home-office desk marked NA."

"I'll take care of it," she said and grabbed the manila envelope. Stopping in her bedroom—her old bedroom, she mentally corrected herself—she ran a brush through her hair and put on some lip gloss. She gave a quick glance in the mirror and surprised herself with her image. Her eyes sparkled, her cheeks were flushed with excitement and her lips curved in a smile.

Because of Rafe? she wondered. She decided, for once, not to second guess herself. She was happy. Joel was happy and she wanted to help make Rafe happy.

She hopped into the town car and followed the instructions from the GPS to Rafe's yacht. Valet took care of parking and she walked toward the yacht with the envelope in her hand. The sun shone brightly, matching her mood.

A staff member greeted her, invited her onboard and pointed her in the direction of Rafe's office. Descending the stairs, she heard voices as she drew closer. The door to the office stood ajar.

She pushed it open and found Rafe in Maddie's arms.

"We were always meant to be together," Maddie said, sliding her fingers through his hair and pressing herself against him. "This marriage won't change a thing. You'll never be able to trust her like you can trust me."

Stunned, she dropped the envelope and Rafe immediately looked up at her. "Nicole," he said. "It's not—"

"No," she said, shaking her head and stumbling backward. Her heart felt as if it shattered into a million pieces.

The pain was staggering. "I—I—" Her throat closed around a huge knot of emotion, forcing out a squeak of distress.

Terrified that she would burst into tears, she turned and fled. Blindly climbing stairs, she ran toward the light, wondering when she would breathe again. She brushed past the staff, all the while hearing Rafe call after her.

"Nicole, wait! Nicole."

Hearing him gain on her, she ran faster. She felt like such a fool. There for two nights, she'd believed it was possible that she and Rafe could make their marriage work. Now, she knew better. He was wealthy and successful, so the usual rules didn't apply to him. He was entitled to whatever and whomever he wanted just like her father.

She felt his hand on her arm and she tried to pull away, but he caught her shoulders in a gentle, but firm grasp and turned her to face him. His gaze bore into hers. "You were right about Maddie. I told her you and I got married and she went berserk. She said it was a mistake and that we belonged together. You saw."

"But she said our marriage wouldn't change anything between the two of you," she said, afraid to believe him.

"She was wrong and I'm going to have to dismiss her. She's never crossed that line with me until today."

"You're going to fire her?" she said, not sure whether she should be relieved or feel pity for the woman.

"I don't have a choice," he said. "You and I are just getting started and you and Joel are most important."

She bit her lip, wondering why she believed him. Was it the rock-solid honesty she saw in his eyes? Or was it wishful thinking?

He rubbed his hands over her upper arms. "I don't want you going anywhere right now. I'll take you home," he said.

"Are you sure?" she asked. "Don't you already have your Corvette here?"

"I'll send the chauffeur for it." He raked one of his hands through his hair. "Just give me five minutes. I need to officially dismiss Maddie and have her escorted off the yacht."

"Escorted off?" she repeated, wincing at the implications.

He nodded. "I'll send her a letter of recommendation via email, but she needs to leave immediately. I'll meet you at the valet in five minutes or less." He lowered his head and pressed his mouth to hers, his kiss providing a reminder of promises they'd made so recently.

She walked along the dock toward the valet, feeling a stab of sympathy for Maddie. Rafe was irresistible. Heaven knew, she had tried not to fall for him, but his combination of strength and drive, not just for business, but for Joel, had made something inside her shift. Maybe everything inside her had shifted, she thought as she turned and saw Rafe striding toward her. Her heart stuttered.

"Is she okay?" she asked as he stepped beside her and guided her the rest of the way to the valet.

He asked for the car and turned to her, shaking his head and lifting a strand of her hair. "You're incredibly beautiful on the outside, Nicole, and your heart is just as beautiful."

She felt a crazy thrill at his words. "What do you mean?"

"I mean you just walked in on a woman trying to steal your husband of two days and you're concerned about her welfare. That's pretty damn exceptional to me."

"I feel sorry for her. I try to imagine working for you all these years and hiding my true feelings. You're very difficult for women."

He tilted his head and wrinkled his brow. "Difficult?" he echoed, helping her into the passenger side of the Lincoln. He climbed into the driver's side and closed his door. "Difficult?"

"Well, yes," she said as he shifted the car into gear and accelerated. "You're good-looking, successful, charming and considerate. How is a woman to resist?"

He pulled the car to a stop. "Are you telling me you can't resist me?"

She opened her mouth then closed it. "You don't need me to feed your ego."

"Yes, I do. I'm starving," he said, flirting outrageously.

She glanced out the window to hide her smile. "I somehow think you'll survive."

Twelve

The only thing better than teasing Nicole was having sex with her. A discerning woman if ever there was one, Rafe felt as if he'd won a prize by earning a portion of her trust. He had far to go, but he was determined. From the devotion she showed Joel and the way she'd already given herself to Rafe, he knew she was a once-in-a-lifetime kind of woman. He was determined to win her mind, body and soul.

As they pulled into the driveway, Rafe noticed another car. "I wonder who it is. Did you schedule any appointments this afternoon?"

"None," she said, shaking her head. "You don't think one of your clients could have gotten confused and decided to try to meet you here?"

He shook his head, thinking of the conference call he'd made this morning to seal his latest deal. "No. I was wrapping up some details just before Maddie ambushed me." He killed the engine. "Let's see who it is."

After they got out of the car, he slid his arm around her waist and walked into the house. Carol immediately appeared. "Mr. Conrad Livingstone is here. He said he was Nicole's father, so I let him in."

Rafe looked at Nicole. Her face turned ashen. "It's okay," he said. "I'll tell him to leave."

"Do you think—" she began.

Mr. Livingstone, a tall, distinguished-looking man with a good ol' boy Southern accent, strolled into the foyer. "Well, well, how do you do it?" he drawled. "Take both of my daughters to bed and steal my deal with the Argyros Cruise Line?"

Rage rolled through Rafe. Instinctively, he pulled back his arm, winding up for a punch to the man's face.

Nicole covered his arm. "No."

He blinked, taking a breath, itching—with every fiber of his being—to wipe the smile off the bastard's face.

"If you hit him, you're no better than he is," she said in a low voice.

He took another breath to try to calm himself and lowered his fist. "First, don't speak that way to my wife," Rafe said, and watched Livingstone's composure slip.

"Second, I won that deal because I worked it better than you did," Rafe said.

Nicole looked up at him. "Is this the Greek deal I told you about?"

Rafe nodded. "I'd been talking to the same company."

"You bastard," Livingstone said.

"Not bastard," Rafe said, checking his anger. "Orphan, but not bastard. You can leave now."

"Not without my daughter and grandson." Livingstone

looked at Nicole. "Surely you can't trust this man. You know you're just a substitute for Tabitha," he said.

Rafe's anger flared again. "Shut—"

"The only reason he wants you is because you have Joel. He's just using you," Nicole's father said.

"That's a lie," Rafe said. "Nicole is the best thing that ever happened to me."

Nicole did a double take.

"He's just saying that so he can keep Joel. He wants control of Joel's inheritance."

Nicole shook her head. "That doesn't make sense. Rafe has plenty of money of his own."

Rafe felt a swell of pride.

"The only reason he wants you and Joel is to get revenge against me because I broke up him and Tabitha."

Until then, Nicole had stood firm, but that last dart appeared to have hit the target dead-on. She bit her lip and closed her eyes as if she were trying to gather her sense, her composure.

"Nicole, he doesn't know what he's talking about," Rafe said in a low voice, slid his hand around her back. She stiffened against his touch. The slight movement wounded him. "Nicole."

She lifted her hands.

"Nicole, I'm your father. I'm Joel's grandfather. Surely you wouldn't want to deprive him of his heritage as a Livingstone. I'll take care of you. I've always been there for you," he said. "Where was Medici when Joel was born? When Tabitha died?"

Rafe clenched his fists at his sides in controlled fury.

She closed her eyes and he sensed her wavering. It stabbed at his gut.

"Do you know what a coup it is for someone like him to associate with a Livingstone?" her father goaded.

A long silence passed and Rafe had the sensation of hanging over a pit of snakes. Would Nicole really go to her father?

She finally opened her eyes. "Rafe couldn't be there because he didn't know Joel existed. You made sure of that, didn't you?"

"I told Tabitha that if she didn't break up with him, then I would take away her trust fund. It was for her good. Even you know she was impulsive. She didn't fight me," he said, giving Rafe a condescending look. "I told you before he just wants you as a substitute for Tabitha. He just wants Joel to get back at me."

She flinched then seemed to stiffen. "That's where you're wrong. Maybe I'm only a substitute, but he wants to be a father to Joel. It's very important to him. He loves Joel and would do anything to protect him."

"I would protect Joel," her father said.

She shook her head. "Only until he displeased you," she said. "Joel and I will never live with you. I'm not going back with you."

Livingstone's face turned to stone. "You'll regret it. Are you so desperate that you're willing to be your sister's stand-in?"

"Get out," Rafe said. He refused to allow her to suffer one second longer.

"Who do you think you are?" Livingstone said. "Giving me orders."

"You're in my house and I want you out. I'll call security if necessary."

"Not man enough to do it yourself," Nicole's father goaded.

"Nicole is too important to me to resort to violence with her father. Get out," he commanded.

As Conrad Livingstone stalked out the front door, Nicole wrapped her arms around herself, her eyes dark with turbulent emotion.

Rafe put his hand on her arm, but she backed away, not meeting his gaze. "I need to pick up Joel," she said. "I don't want to be late."

"I'll go with you," he said.

"No," she said quickly. "I need a few moments to myself."

"Are you sure you should drive?" he asked.

She nodded. "Yes. I'll be fine. I just need some air," she said and lifted her hands for the keys.

He pressed them into her palm and watched her walk out of the door. He couldn't help wondering if he'd just lost his last chance with the only woman who'd ever made him feel like he'd found home just by holding her in his arms.

Nicole wanted to take Joel and run. Driving to pick him up at preschool, she felt as if she'd been punched.

The deal with the Greek shipping company. When had that really happened? Had she blown her father's deal by unwittingly giving information to Rafe? Even though she wanted distance from her father, she wished him no ill will.

Her father's worst accusation was that she was a fill-in for Tabitha. In other circumstances, she could have stood it. After all, she'd spent most of her life in the shadow of her sister. But now, now she wanted Rafe to see *her*, to want *her*, to love *her*.

Her breath stopped in her throat. Even though he was

the strongest man she'd ever met, she wanted to make him feel safe. She wanted to make his secret wishes come true. She wanted him to feel her love. And she wanted to feel loved by him.

Panic coursed through her. What an idiot, she thought, pulling into a parking spot at the preschool. Rafe had made it clear that love wasn't part of the bargain.

An hour and a half later, Rafe was swearing as he paced his downstairs office. With the exception of the tragedy of his father's death and mother's subsequent decline, he'd felt as if he'd usually held the lucky side of the coin. Not with love, of course, but with business. Today, he felt as if the bad luck gods had decided to pummel him. First the incident with Maddie, then Nicole's father. He rubbed his hand across his face as he paced and swore under his breath. How in the world could he make this right for Nicole? How could he make her believe what she meant to him? .

Nicole and Joel had become as vital to him as his heart and lungs. The reality of their importance took his breath away.

"Mr. Medici," Carol said, holding a manila envelope in her hands. "I apologize for the interruption."

Rafe glanced up at his longtime housekeeper. "Yes?"

"Unfortunately, my new housekeeping assistant broke a vase of flowers in Mrs. Medici's bedroom. Her previous bedroom, that is. The water spilled into the drawer all over this envelope. I wasn't sure if it was important." She extended the envelope toward him and he took it.

"Thank you. I'll look it over." He opened the envelope and pulled out the printed copy of the investigator's report on him, along with two passports. Frowning, he flipped each open, seeing first a photo of Nicole, then one of Joel.

Flipping through the papers, he stopped cold when he saw a listing of international flight departures from Miami and requirements for taking a minor out of the country.

Rafe felt as if he'd been stabbed in the heart.

Nicole had been planning to take Joel away.

From his office, he heard the front door burst open.

"Daddy!" Joel called.

His son's voice twisted his gut. "In here," he said, keeping his own voice level for the sake of Joel.

Nicole and Joel walked inside, chomping down the remnants of ice cream cones. Nicole offered him a cup of ice cream. Rafe was so furious he could have melted the frozen treat just by looking at it. They'd been eating ice cream when he'd been sweating blood.

He put his hands on his hips and looked at both of them. "Someone's been having fun."

Lifting her shoulders, Nicole smiled vaguely. "It seemed like a good day for ice cream."

Joel gave a big nod. "Every day is a good day for ice cream. I petted a turtle."

"Yeah?" Rafe said, focusing on his son. "What did you think of him?"

"He was cool, but I'd rather have a gerbil. That's what we get to pet next week."

Rafe raised his eyebrows. "Really? You'll have to tell us about that. What do you want to do now, buddy? Swim?"

"I wanna do more than dog paddle."

"That's my boy. Go get your swim trunks on," he said and Joel vanished upstairs. Rafe turned to Nicole. "You and I will talk later."

Her smile fell and her face turned serious. "What do you mean?" she asked.

He pressed the manila envelope along with the papers into her hands. "I mean, you and I will be making new arrangements," he said and left her as he went upstairs to change into his swim trunks. He left the small cup of ice cream untouched on his desk.

Nicole stared at the passports and flight plans and her stomach sank to her feet. A damning shame fell over her. After she'd left to pick up Joel, Rafe had probably wondered if she planned to take their son and flee the country. Swamped with remorse, she covered her face. She'd researched those flights just after she'd received the investigator's report about Rafe. She'd put together those contingency plans weeks ago.

The more she'd learned about Rafe, the more certain she'd been that she couldn't take his son from him. As Rafe and Joel grew closer, she knew it would also devastate her son. Despite all her doubts, she'd known she had to help Rafe become the father both he and Joel needed him to be.

Now Rafe was furious, and she didn't know what she could do about it. How could she fix this?

Hours later, after he'd worn out Joel and the cook prepared pasta, Rafe and Nicole put Joel to bed. Leaving Joel's room, Rafe shut the door behind him. "It's time to talk," he said and led the way downstairs.

Nicole's stomach twisted into a dozen knots. How could she explain? Even if she could, how could he possibly believe?

As soon as they reached the den, he turned toward her. "When were you planning to take him?"

She bit her lip. "I know you won't believe this, but taking Joel was just a back-up plan. I had to make sure you wouldn't hurt him. Between what Tabitha had told me and the investigator's report, I had to be ready to do whatever was necessary to keep Joel safe."

He nodded, his eyes as cold as ice. "You're right," he said. "I don't believe you. It's too convenient. Since marrying me, you gained shared custody of Joel."

"You have to remember that I had full custody before you showed up only a month ago," she shot back.

"That was based on false pretenses," he said. "Tabitha lied by not putting my name on the birth certificate and you were going to use that to your advantage."

"Only if necessary," Nicole said. "Only if you were abusive."

His eyes turned black with anger. "But I never was," he told her. "You can have the master bedroom. I'll go back to the yacht."

Her heart twisted in her chest. "No," she said impulsively. "Keep your room. Joel needs to see you as much as possible. I'll move back into my old room."

Rafe paused then nodded, "Fine."

Nicole felt something inside her shrivel. Hope. Unfortunately, it wasn't love. Heaven help her, she still loved Rafe with everything inside her.

Days and nights passed with Rafe ignoring her at every turn. Nicole didn't know if she could bear his banked antipathy toward her. He hated her, but understood that Joel needed her. Therefore, he allowed her to stay.

Nicole struggled to find a way to make the situation better for all three of them. She even wondered if she should leave. The very thought of it tore her apart.

After Joel went to bed one night, she confronted Rafe. "Do you want me to leave?"

He shook his head. "No. I want you to stay. My son needs you."

But not Rafe. Her stomach twisted. She sucked in a shallow breath. "I talked to a lawyer. I'm signing back full custody to you and I'm proposing an annulment for our marriage."

Rafe stared at her in cynical surprise. "Annulment?" he echoed. "We consummated our marriage on the way home from the so-called ceremony."

His words lashed at her. She cringed, but took another breath, determined to do everything she could to make the situation right. "If we annul the marriage, then I won't share custody of Joel and you won't owe me anything. No money. Nothing. Ever."

He narrowed his eyes. "You would give up all your rights?"

"Yes," she whispered.

"I'll think about it," he said with a careless shrug, and she knew she'd lost him forever.

Thirteen

Each day that Nicole spent in Rafe's house was harder than the last. She'd thought it would get easier. It had to, she told herself every night and every morning, but it hadn't. With a mixture of relief and sadness, she accepted her cousin Julia's invitation to attend her baby's christening. Julia had also asked Nicole to be the baby's godmother. In light of how Nicole has messed up her current situation, she was thankful for Julia's confidence in her.

"I'm going back to Atlanta next weekend," she told Rafe that evening after another meal where he barely spoke to her.

He paused and looked at her. "For how long?"

"Just for the weekend. Julia's baby is being christened."

"Okay, but you won't be taking Joel," he said.

"I hadn't planned on taking Joel," she said, unable to keep a twinge of defensiveness from her tone. "I knew you wouldn't want him to go. I know you don't trust me."

"On the contrary, I trust you very much when it comes to the care of my son, or you would be out of my house."

His words shouldn't have stabbed at her, but they did. Rising from the table, she met his gaze. "Well, I'll be out of your house next weekend. Maybe that will do both of us some good," she said, then turned to go.

She barely took a step before she felt his hand close around her wrist. "What do you mean by that?" he demanded.

She couldn't make herself look at him. "I know you don't understand how I could have made those back-up plans to protect Joel—"

"How you could take him away from his father, from his home," he said, his voice full of emotion.

She closed her eyes to contain herself. "The reason you'll never understand is because your father wasn't abusive and you lost him and your home. That's all you can see. I wish, for one moment, just one moment that you could pretend my father was your father and he'd abused you."

Silence followed and Nicole felt herself tremble.

"It still doesn't change—"

A crushing disappointment pushed down on her and she stepped away from Rafe, pulling her hand from his. "That's what makes it so hard," she said, forcing herself to look at him. "Nothing is going to change. And I did this other very stupid thing that I wish I could change, but it's not happening."

He frowned at her. "What other stupid thing?"

She gave a wry laugh that hid a sob. "In spite of all the warnings from Tabitha, from Maddie, from my father, I went and fell—" She broke off. "Do you know how hard it is to stay in this house married to you knowing that you hate me?" She shook her head. "I'm going to my room."

"Nicole," he said, catching her hand again and the warmth of his hand reminded her of all the warmth they'd begun to share, but lost.

She shook her head. "Let me go," she said, wishing her voice wasn't so obviously full of tears. "I've said too much."

The following Friday evening, Nicole flew to Atlanta, leaving Rafe with Joel. Rafe noticed his son pacing to the front windows then back to the den where Joel's favorite cartoon was on television.

"Everything okay?" Rafe asked, looking up from his newspaper.

Joel nodded, sitting on the sofa, but swinging his legs restlessly. "I wonder if Mom is with Aunt Julia and baby Sidney."

Rafe glanced at his watch. Nicole had insisted on flying coach even though he'd offered the use of his jet. "Her plane was supposed to arrive thirty minutes ago, so I'm sure she's on her way to your aunt's house."

"She said she'd call me when she gets there," Joel said, crossing his arms over his chest.

"She will."

"She's gonna be a godmother to Sidney, but that's not a real mother. She'll still be my real mother," Joel said.

"Always," Rafe said. "Come here and sit with me," he said.

Joel jumped off the couch and climbed into Rafe's lap. Rafe felt a flood of love and protectiveness for his son. He was so young, so vulnerable. Rafe would do anything to keep his Joel safe.

He could tell that Joel missed Nicole. What surprised Rafe was his own sense that something was wrong in the house since she'd left. It was his house for Pete's sake, so he should be fine with her not there. In fact, he should be relieved. Without her around, he wasn't reminded of what she'd done. He wasn't reminded of the fact that they were married in name only. He wasn't reminded of her sexy sweetness and the way she'd once made him believe he could have what he'd always longed for with her and Joel.

In the two weeks since their wedding, he'd expected to see resentment in her eyes. Instead, he'd glimpsed her pain. Plus, she'd offered to give up all her rights, all the money he'd agreed to give her if they divorced. He'd thought it was a ploy. Now he wasn't so sure.

Joel laid his head against Rafe's chest and gave a heavy sigh. Thirty minutes later, his son was asleep. Rafe carefully shifted him in his arms and carried him upstairs. He considered putting him to bed without brushing his teeth, but knew Nicole would have his hide.

After Rafe helped Joel get ready for bed, his son pulled out a book about animal mommies. Halfway through the book, his cell rang. Checking the caller ID, he saw that it was Nicole and his heart stumbled oddly. "Hi," he said.

"Hi. Thanks for picking up. I promised Joel I would call him."

"Here he is," Rafe said and held the phone against Joel's ear. Joel chatted with her for a moment, asking about baby Sidney and Aunt Julia.

"Yes, I've been good. Daddy and I had pizza." He paused a moment. "I love you, too, Mommy."

"Let me talk to her once more," Rafe said in a low voice.

"Here's Daddy," Joel said.

"I can still send my personal jet to bring you back," Rafe offered.

"No. It's really not necessary," she said. "After all, it's a direct flight. The chauffeur can pick me up."

"Okay," he said. "Take care of yourself."

She paused. "You, too."

Joel picked up the book again for Rafe to finish. "I have the best mom in the world," he said, rubbing his eyes and slinking against Rafe. "She reads me lots of books and she plays games with me. She gives me hugs. She's not very good at Wii, though."

Rafe chuckled. "Nobody's perfect."

"She's almost perfect," Joel said and reached up to give Rafe a hug. "Are we gonna live here forever?"

Rafe sucked in a deep breath at the hope in his son's eyes. "Do you like it here?"

Joel nodded. "I like the pool," he said. "And you're good at Wii."

Rafe cradled his son against him. "I like having you here," he muttered.

Joel sighed and yawned. "You give good hugs, too. G'night."

"G'night," Rafe echoed and turned off the bedside lamp. He glanced back at his son before he left the room and the second he stepped into the hall, he felt a shocking loneliness. When had it happened? When had his desire for Nicole turned to need? He'd been so angry he'd denied the possibility of feeling anything but betrayal.

It suddenly hit Rafe that despite her doubts and worries, she had done everything she possibly could to help Rafe forge a good relationship with his son. She had backed him with the social services specialist. She'd believed in him when she'd walked in on that ridiculous scene with Maddie, and she'd stayed with him despite all the terrible things her father had said about him. She could have left. A hundred times, she could have left, but she hadn't.

As if someone washed the mud off his glasses, he saw things differently. Rafe realized that when he'd rejected Nicole, he had turned away the most precious thing in his life.

Raking his fingers through his hair, he searched for a way to repair the damage. She'd looked so broken this afternoon before she'd left. Resolved, but miserable.

He'd done that to her. What good had it done? In punishing her, he was punishing himself. Swearing under his breath, he wondered if he'd lost the chance of a lifetime.

Nicole took her seat in the front chapel pew as Julia held Sidney and her husband chatted with the chaplain at the front. A small group of family friends filled the small chapel.

Tears filled her eyes at the love Julia and her husband shared. Julia was so lucky. Nicole would never know that kind of love from her husband. She pulled a tissue from her purse, wishing she weren't so emotional. If she remained married to Rafe, she'd probably never have another child. The thought stabbed at her like a hot coal.

She gave herself a stern kick in the butt. She needed to stop feeling sorry for herself. After all, she was honored that Julia had chosen her as Sidney's godmother.

The sound of footsteps distracted her and she looked up to find Rafe and Joel walking toward her. Shock coursed through her and she stood. "Is everything okay?" she asked Rafe, glancing again at Joel. "Is he—"

"He's fine," Rafe said. "I just decided that you should have your husband and son by your side when you become a godmother.

She dropped her jaw. "How did you—"

"I have a jet," he said, touching her arm and guiding her to sit down. "Remember?"

Joel rushed to give her a hug. "Why is Sidney's dress so long?" he asked in a loud whisper.

"It's called a christening gown. That's what they look like," she said and smiled. "I missed you."

He gave her another hug and sat on the other side of her. She noticed Rafe extended his arm across the back of the pew, just touching her shoulders and wondered what was going on. "I don't understand."

"We'll talk later," he said.

She studied his gaze and for the first time in weeks, saw no anger. Her heart stuttered.

"Welcome to each of you," the chaplain said. "We're here to give thanks and celebrate our joy at the arrival of this precious child."

Nicole focused on the ceremony, but was distracted by Rafe's presence, the way he looked at her. She could almost think he wanted— She broke off the thought, afraid to hope.

Afterward, the small group adjourned to Julia and her husband's home for a casual gathering with finger foods. Julia greeted Rafe. "I didn't think you were coming. What a surprise."

"Last-minute decision. I hope you don't mind," Rafe said.

"Not at all," she said, her gaze bouncing between Rafe and Nicole. She glanced at Joel, who was building a LEGO castle with another child. "Joel looks occupied. I think I left a couple of gifts in the car. Would you two mind getting them for me?"

"Of course," Nicole said and led the way to the driveway. She rubbed her hands over her arms, the cool temperature taking her by surprise.

Rafe replaced her hands with his, shocking the living daylights out of her. "You've already gotten used to the Miami warmth," he said.

She nodded, her heart hammering against her ribcage. "I guess I have."

"I've been wrong," he said.

Nicole didn't think he could have surprised her any further, but he just had. She sucked in a mind-clearing breath. "Excuse me?"

"I said I've been wrong."

Nicole blinked. "I never even imagined those words coming out of your mouth."

One side of his mouth lifted in a cryptic grin, but his eyes remained serious. "When I found out you'd made plans to take Joel out of the country—"

"Back-up plans," she had to remind him, because she'd never imagined how she could go through with them.

He dipped his head. "Back-up plans. I was so angry," he said. "Terrified."

She made an audible gulp.

"I finally had what I'd wanted my whole life and it could have been gone like that. The possibility that you could take away everything important to me just—" He took a deep breath. "You haven't just been Joel's dream mom. You've been my dream woman."

Nicole gasped and shook her head.

He nodded. "Your father was wrong," he said. "You're no replacement for Tabitha. I don't want to be disrespectful, but you're so much more. You've turned my life around in a good way."

"Oh, I hope you mean that," she said.

"I do."

"Because I've fallen in love with you," she said.

Rafe's heart stopped. "Do you realize what you just said?" he asked.

She nodded. "It's one of those things that was bursting to come out, but I was so afraid to say it. I know you don't feel the same way, but—"

"Whoa," he said. "How do you know I don't feel the same way?"

She met his gaze then looked away. "You said you didn't believe in love."

"Give me a chance to recover from emotional whiplash, sweetheart. I've never met anyone like you. You make me want to be your only man, your protector, your everything."

She sucked in a quick breath. "You are."

He closed his eyes and twined his fingers through hers. "I never knew what love really was until you came into my life," he said, then opened his eyes. "I love you, Nicole. I've wanted and needed you in my life before I even met you."

Her eyes grew shiny with unshed tears. "I love you and I will do anything to protect you."

He squeezed out a hoarse chuckle. When had any woman said she would protect him? "I'm the luckiest man in the world," he said, lowering his lips to hers.

"You just made all my dreams come true," she said, murmuring against his mouth.

"There's more Nic," he said. "So much more. And we're going to spend the rest of our lives together."

Three weeks later, Nicole shared a large, comfy chaise lounge with Rafe by the pool after Joel went to bed. With her back resting against his and her head tucked beneath his shoulder, she couldn't imagine a better place in the world to be.

His hands wrapped around her, making her feel surrounded by him. She sighed, looking up at the stars.

"Happy?" he asked, his lips brushing her forehead.

She smiled and closed her eyes, savoring the moment. "Yes, and you?"

"More than I ever dreamed," he said.

She turned to lift her lips for a kiss. She intended it to be a quick caress, but Rafe clearly wanted more. Nicole didn't mind at all. When he pulled back, she looked into his eyes and shivered at how incredibly lucky she was.

Leaning back against his chest, she lifted his hand and stroked his wide palm. "As much as I love you and I know you love me, there's still a lot we don't know about each other."

"Like what?" he asked.

"Well, I want you to get enough time on your yacht in the ocean because I know it makes you feel better. How much time do you need?"

"Not as much as I used to," he said, lifting his hand to play with her hair. "I feel better when I'm with you and Joel."

She nodded. "And what about travel? What's the maximum time you think you would be gone?"

"No more than a week," he said. "Two, tops. In either case, I may just have to drag you and Joel along with me."

"Did you ever have a pet as a child?" she asked, gradually working her way to the topic most important to her.

"We had a stray dog before my father died, but had to give it up when my mother let us go," he told her.

Another loss, she thought and lifted his hand to her mouth to comfort him. "Did you help take care of it?"

"Yep. We took turns. Why? Does Joel want a dog? I'm okay with it," he said.

"That's good," she said absently. "Have you ever changed a diaper?"

He paused. "Not that I can remember. Why?"

"Well, you know, I'm a godmother and Julia may want to leave Sidney with us sometime so she and her husband can take a little break." She turned slightly to look up at him. "Would you be willing to help?"

"With diapers?" he asked.

She nodded. "And if she should get up in the night. And giving her a bath."

He cleared his throat. "I may need some training, but hell, yeah. Why not?"

She smiled, lifting her head. "I'm glad to hear it."

"The diaper thing may not be my favorite," he said.

"But you're still willing to help?"

He nodded. "Yeah."

"That's good," she said. "Because I'm pregnant."

He blinked. "What?"

"I'm pregnant," she repeated.

"But I think we just had that one time without protection," he said, staring at her in disbelief.

"Right, and you said something about people don't necessarily get pregnant from just one time. Well, we did."

He continued to stare at her for several seconds.

Nicole felt a ripple of nerves. "This is when you say, *Sweetheart, this is great news. You've made me the happiest man in the world.*"

He opened his mouth then shut it. "You took the words right out of my mouth."

She gave him a soft punch. "Lame, lame, lame."

He slid his hands through her hair and looked at her in amazement. "Are you sure?"

She nodded. "Two e.p.t tests and I went to the doctor this morning."

He closed his eyes then opened them. If she didn't know better, she would say that her type A, tough-guy husband's eyes had a sheen of moisture. "How do you feel about it?"

"I'm so happy I almost can't stand it," she whispered.

"I love you, Nicole. I can't wait to be with you every step of the way through this. Every step, every day. You keep making my dreams come true."

* * * * *

*Don't miss THE PLAYBOY'S PROPOSITION,
the next MEDICI MEN romance from
USA Today bestselling author Leanne Banks
On sale February 9, 2010
from Silhouette Desire*

"AREN'T YOU GOING TO SAY 'Fly me' or at least 'Welcome Aboard'?"

Amanda Bauer didn't. The softly muttered word that actually came out of her mouth was a lot less welcoming. And had fewer letters. Four, to be exact.

The man shook his head and tsked. "Not exactly the friendly skies. Haven't caught the spirit yet this morning?"

"Make one more airline-slogan crack and you'll be walking to Chicago," she said.

He nodded once, then pushed his sunglasses onto the top of his tousled hair. The move revealed blue eyes that matched the sky above. And yeah. They were twinkling. Damn it.

"Understood. Just, uh, promise me you'll say 'Coffee, tea or me' at least once, okay? Please?"

Amanda tried to glare, but that twinkle sucked the annoyance right out of her. She could only draw in a slow breath as he climbed into the plane. As she watched her passenger disappear into the small jet, she had to wonder about the trip she was about to take.

Coffee and tea they had, and he was welcome to them. But her? Well, she'd never even considered making a move on a customer before. Talk about unprofessional.

And yet…

Something inside her suddenly wanted to take a chance, to be a little outrageous.

How long since she had done indecent things—or decent ones, for that matter—with a sexy man? Not since before they'd thrown all their energies into expanding Clear-Blue Air, at the very least. She hadn't had time for a lunch date, much less the kind of lust-fest she'd enjoyed in her younger years. The kind that lasted for entire weekends and involved not leaving a bed except to grab the kind of sensuous food that could be smeared onto—and eaten off—someone else's hot, naked, sweat-tinged body.

She closed her eyes, her hand clenching tight on the railing. Her heart fluttered in her chest and she tried to make herself move. But she couldn't—not climbing up, but not backing away, either. Not physically, and not in her head.

Was she really considering this? God, she hadn't even looked at the stranger's left hand to make sure he was available. She had no idea if he was actually attracted to her or just an irrepressible flirt. Yet something inside was telling her to take a shot with this man.

It was crazy. Something she'd never considered. Yet right now, at this moment, she was definitely considering it. If he was available…could she do it? Seduce a stranger. Have an anonymous fling, like something out of a blue movie on late-night cable?

She didn't know. All she knew was that the flight to Chicago was a short one so she had to decide quickly. And as she put her foot on the bottom step and began to climb up, Amanda suddenly had to wonder if she was about to embark on the ride of her life.

HARLEQUIN® *Blaze*™

*It all started
with a few naughty books....*

As a member of the Red Tote Book Club,
Carol Snow has been studying works of
classic erotic literature...but Carol doesn't
believe in love...or marriage. It's going to take
another kind of classic—Charles Dickens's
A Christmas Carol—and a little otherworldly
persuasion to convince her to go after her
own sexily ever after.

Cuddle up with

Her Sexy Valentine

by STEPHANIE BOND

Available February 2010

_____

red-hot reads

www.eHarlequin.com

HB79526

HARLEQUIN
Ambassadors

Want to share your passion for reading Harlequin® Books?

Become a Harlequin Ambassador!

Harlequin Ambassadors are a group
of passionate and well-connected readers
who are willing to share their joy of reading
Harlequin® books with family and friends.

You'll be sent all the tools you need to spark
great conversation, including free books!

All we ask is that you share the romance
with your friends and family!

You'll also be invited to have a say in
new book ideas and exchange opinions
with women just like you!

To see if you qualify* to be
a Harlequin Ambassador, please visit
www.HarlequinAmbassadors.com.

*Please note that not everyone who applies to be a Harlequin Ambassador will
qualify. For more information please visit www.HarlequinAmbassadors.com.

Thank you for your participation.

BAP09BPA

HARLEQUIN® HISTORICAL:
Where love is timeless

From chivalrous knights
to roguish rakes, look for the
variety Harlequin® Historical
has to offer every month.

www.eHarlequin.com

PREGNANT BRIDES

*Inexperienced and expecting,
they're forced to marry!*

Bestselling Harlequin Presents author

Lynne Graham

brings you the second story
in this exciting new trilogy:

RUTHLESS MAGNATE,
CONVENIENT WIFE
#2892
Available February 2010

Also look for

GREEK TYCOON,
INEXPERIENCED MISTRESS
#2900
Available March 2010

www.eHarlequin.com

HP12892

REQUEST YOUR FREE BOOKS!

2 FREE NOVELS
PLUS 2
FREE GIFTS!

Passionate, Powerful, Provocative!

YES! Please send me 2 FREE Silhouette Desire® novels and my 2 FREE gifts (gifts are worth about $10). After receiving them, if I don't wish to receive any more books, I can return the shipping statement marked "cancel." If I don't cancel, I will receive 6 brand-new novels every month and be billed just $4.05 per book in the U.S. or $4.74 per book in Canada. That's a saving of almost 15% off the cover price! It's quite a bargain! Shipping and handling is just 50¢ per book in the U.S. and 75¢ per book in Canada.* I understand that accepting the 2 free books and gifts places me under no obligation to buy anything. I can always return a shipment and cancel at any time. Even if I never buy another book, the two free books and gifts are mine to keep forever.

225 SDN E39X 326 SDN E4AA

Name _____ (PLEASE PRINT)

Address _____ Apt. #

City _____ State/Prov. _____ Zip/Postal Code

Signature (if under 18, a parent or guardian must sign)

Mail to the Silhouette Reader Service:

IN U.S.A.: P.O. Box 1867, Buffalo, NY 14240-1867
IN CANADA: P.O. Box 609, Fort Erie, Ontario L2A 5X3

Not valid for current subscribers to Silhouette Desire books.

Want to try two free books from another line?
Call 1-800-873-8635 or visit www.morefreebooks.com.

* Terms and prices subject to change without notice. Prices do not include applicable taxes. N.Y. residents add applicable sales tax. Canadian residents will be charged applicable provincial taxes and GST. Offer not valid in Quebec. This offer is limited to one order per household. All orders subject to approval. Credit or debit balances in a customer's account(s) may be offset by any other outstanding balance owed by or to the customer. Please allow 4 to 6 weeks for delivery. Offer available while quantities last.

Your Privacy: Silhouette Books is committed to protecting your privacy. Our Privacy Policy is available online at www.eHarlequin.com or upon request from the Reader Service. From time to time we make our lists of customers available to reputable third parties who may have a product or service of interest to you. If you would prefer we not share your name and address, please check here. ☐

Help us get it right—We strive for accurate, respectful and relevant communications. To clarify or modify your communication preferences, visit us at www.ReaderService.com/consumerschoice.

SDES10

Money can't buy him love…
but it can get his foot in the door

He needed a wife…fast. And Texan Jeff Brand's
lovely new assistant would do just fine. After all,
the heat between him and Holly Lombard was
becoming impossible to resist. And a no-strings
marriage would certainly work for them both—
but will he be able to keep his feelings out of
this in-name-only union?

Find out in

MARRYING
THE LONE STAR
MAVERICK

by *USA TODAY* bestselling author
SARA ORWIG

Available in February

Always Powerful, Passionate and Provocative!